HUNTED FOR Christmas

DES SWEET

First published by: Des Sweet

Editor: Jasmine Acena

Developmental Editor/Alpha Reader: Megan Henry

Cover Design: Artscandare

Chapter headers designed in Canva

Contents

Content Warning

Warning the content of the content warning is too disturbing to print.

This is a PITCH BLACK DARK STALKER ROMANCE

The content is not suitable for society. Proceed at your own risk.

Hunted for Christmas will not only ruin food for you, but it will make you question what you just read.

By ignoring this page you agree to hold me and my team harmless from any future therapy you might require. To included but not limited to: book boyfriend envy. We can not be responsible for your depraved disregard for serious and not at all annoying warnings.

If you made it this far then you probably hate surprises and take warnings seriously, <u>you can read the full warning here on my website.</u>

Dedication

For all the dark romantics who fantasize about being...

Hunted for Christmas

XoXo

—Kane

Hazel

Chapter 1

Ice crunches beneath the car's tires as it slips and slides across the road, narrowly missing careening into a rocky mountainside. Snow-covered pine trees glare at me in the distance, as if whispering a silent warning. A gust of wind slams against the car, sending snow swirling around, clouding my vision. The mountains can be treacherous this time of year—that was a close call. It's not just freezing to death I have to worry about; any small impact from the car could trigger an avalanche of snow to come sliding down the mountainside. I tighten my grip on the steering wheel and take a deep breath before accelerating slowly into danger, continuing my climb up the snowy road to the exit. Inside, I'm a turmoil of emotions. The radio station cut out miles ago, leaving me alone with nothing but my thoughts while my phone charges in the cup holder—safety tip 101 from my father. I can't risk a dead battery if anything should happen while I'm driving.

Thinking about him makes me smile. It's been years since I visited the cozy little mountain town where I'm headed. I vaguely remember summer vacations—days were spent splashing in the cool lake water and evenings we gathered around a bonfire toasting marshmallows while swapping wild, scary stories. But after my grandfather passed away, everything changed. My dad and uncle stopped speaking, unless it was to shout over grandfather's estate and who was to blame for his sudden death. Grief tore their relationship apart. Years later, when my aunt died in a boating accident, they finally made up. It would prove to be too little too late, or just in the nick of time, depending on who you asked. Of course, by then, I was no longer a child. My imagination had been traded for a cell phone, and my toys for a diploma. The thought of spending summers in a small town with spotty reception held no appeal. Exploring the world with my friends—falling in love with a man I thought was the one—consumed all my time. As a result, my relationship with my uncle was fractured at best. I never had the chance to grow up knowing him the way I should have. I squandered my second chance to really get to know him. If I could take it all back now, I would. But Uncle Dex would want me not to be too hard on myself. After his diagnosis, I spent as much time as possible with him, trying to make up for all those years we lost together. Maybe that's why I convinced myself to drive up here, just ahead of a blizzard. A small part of me still feels like I'm making up for lost time. Uncle Dex must have felt the same way—or he wouldn't have left me the cabin in his will. There's just one stipulation to my inheritance of the cabin: I must spend an entire week there in order to establish residency as the new owner.

The attorney for his estate called a few weeks ago to inform me, and the timing couldn't be better. I'm too ashamed of my failed relationship to spend the holidays at my parents' house, and the townhouse just isn't the same without Tyler. Everything feels wrong. The space is a constant reminder of my failure as a partner. But it wasn't me who failed—it was him. There's no coming back from what he did. My heart shattered into a million irreparable pieces, and now I feel numb to the world. A tear rolls down my cheek and I swipe it away. *Now is not the time to get emotional.* The last thing I need is to make my eyes all puffy and drive the car into a ditch—or worse, off the side of the mountain.

A knot forms in my throat at the thought, and I blink, straining to see through the whirling white wisps of snow. Inheriting this old cabin is the gift of space I need this year. I need to get away—to clear my head and really think about how to move on. I'm ready to fall in love, but I refuse to be anything less than his entire world. I want to be adored. I want to wake up every day and know that he's thinking of me because he's just as in love with me as I am with him. I want my happily ever after, goddamn it. And right about now, I'd do just about anything to get one. I'm not above admitting that I secretly hope to find myself in one of those ooey-gooey, mushy holiday romances where the main characters meet and fall in love by Christmas. I may have even planned my entire holiday escape around this delusional fantasy.

In the cup holder, my phone vibrates. I chance a glance at the glowing screen to see who dares to interrupt my holiday alone time so soon. I can only think of one person. My suspicions are confirmed when *Mom* flashes across the screen. Of course, she's checking in. Both she and my dad were worried I didn't leave early enough to beat the storm—and they were right. Now, I'm just hoping I can survive the final fifteen minute stretch of this drive. My exit should be coming up soon, but I can barely see two feet ahead. The phone vibrates again, pulling my eyes from the road. I must be getting better service, which means I am definitely getting close to the exit. When I look down to check the new message, I look up just in time to scare myself senseless. I slam on the brakes, harder than I should. The car fishtails, skidding to a stop with the brakes grinding against the ice. Flashing lights blink right in front of me. *Please don't let the road be closed.* I pray silently, dread creeping in. If the roads are closed, I'm not sure what I'll do. It's not like I have anywhere else to go.

Since I'm stopped for a moment anyway, I snatch up the phone. His name flashes on the screen, sending my heart into a spiral. It's been weeks since he moved to Florida without me—my decision, not his. I toss the phone back into the cupholder, refusing to deal with him right now. I'll be lucky if I make it to the cabin tonight. Whatever he needs has waited weeks, so it can wait a few hours... or even days, if I really feel like it. Resuming my drive, I creep the car forward inch by inch, the car barely crawling as I edge closer to the flashing lights. I flip on my hazards—visibility is awful, and even though I haven't seen another car for miles, the last thing I need is to be rear-ended. At last, I pull up to a police barricade. A single SUV cruiser sits at the bottom of the exit. *Fuck.*

A flashlight waves in the distance, signaling me to stop. I lightly press the brakes, gazing into the snow, waiting for the person to appear. A few minutes later, a shadowy figure emerges, walking slowly up to my car. My stomach churns with nerves as he taps on the window with his flashlight. I roll it down, trying not to panic, though. Why do I have such a bad feeling about this?

"Well, hello there, little lady. What's a sweet thing like you doing out on a night like this—and all alone?" His raspy voice carries a light, awkward chuckle.

My stomach drops. *Lie,* I think to myself. *Lie better than you've ever lied before, Hazel.*

"I, um," I stammer, "I'm just going up the road to my uncle's place. My family's waiting for me there. It's a big tradition. If I don't get there soon, my dad's going to have the entire mountain out looking for me."

"The entire mountain, you don't say?" His tone is skeptical.

I nod feeling the pit in my stomach deepen.

"Look, I'm really sorry, gorgeous, but I'm supposed to close this exit. The roads are getting bad and—" He pauses, thinking. "I suppose I can follow you to your turnoff. 'Tis the season, right?" he chuckles, but it feels forced.

Relief washes over me. Something about his suggestion eases the tension. Maybe I misjudged the situation because I'm stressed over the storm.

"I promise to take it slow, sir," I say, blinking my eyelashes at him, hoping to sway the debate in my favor.

He speaks into his radio, "Sergeant to base."

There's a pause as he listens, then he nods, holding a finger to his ear piece. "Copy. I'm escorting a vehicle up the road, then I'll close the gate behind me. The snow is damn-near impassible. Call in the closure."

"Go on," he says, tipping his head, "I'll be right behind you. Just gotta lock up the gate."

I start to roll my window up, but he stops me by sliding the end of his flashlight into the gap. He leans in, his smile widening. "Now, you stay safe on *my* mountain this weekend, little miss... Jane Doe." The blood in my veins turns to ice as his eyes lock with mine, boring right through me. His good ole boy smile twists into something sinister, and the small sense of safety I had moments ago shatters.

He removes the flashlight, and I quickly roll up my window, pulling past the barrier to be escorted up the mountain. In the rear-view mirror, I barely make out the shape of him as he moves the roadblock into place and locking it. A shudder runs through me realizing exactly why my mother was so worried about me coming up here alone. I really am all alone. An easy target for a predator with no one to protect me. *What if he follows me all the way to the house and realizes I am lying?* Shit. I guess I just need to pray the roads are bad enough he doesn't.

I drive white-knuckled the entire way to the turnoff. He's keeping a decent distance, but it doesn't do much to calm my nerves. My mind is racing as I creep along, the GPS ticks down the miles—and the minutes—until I can finally make the turn.

Thankfully, when I turn down the snow-packed road, the soft glow of his lights disappear into the storm. Around me, endless lines of pine trees stand frozen, their snow-capped branches like icing on a gingerbread house. With no radio, the sound of the tires crunching as they roll over the fresh snow is all I can hear. After several nerve-wracking bends in the road, the GPS dings, indicating the turn onto the private driveway. The cabin comes into view through the falling snow—its peaked roof barely visible against the swirling white flakes spiraling endlessly from the sky. The cabin is so far up the mountain, it feels like I could reach out and touch the clouds in the sky, but it's only a thick layer of fog rolling in with the blizzard. I am surprised to see a soft glow of lights emanating from the front windows when the car tires hit the cement driveway, sliding as I transition from the dirt road onto pavement. *If I remember correctly, the driveway is heated.* I'll have to figure that out tomorrow. Right now, all I want is to collapse into a warm bed and sleep. The estate attorney mentioned a caretaker who lives another mile up the road, and seeing the lights on, I'm hopeful everything is prepared for my stay. I pull the car all the way into the driveway, coasting slowly and carefully up the stretching cement drive to park in front of the garage, relieved to have a garage door opener in my purse. I'm grateful I won't be wrestling a snow-covered door tonight.

I cut the engine and take a deep inhale, letting the crisp mountain air seep into the car. The scent of pine fills my lungs, enveloping my senses, and grounding me. This is it—my first vacation, completely on my own. I grab my overnight bag from the passenger seat, I'm struck by the frigid cold air. The wind whips at my hair, biting at my cheeks as I trudge through the deepening snow drifts to the front door. I climb the wide wooden front steps, holding onto the banister and stomp the snow off my boots with each step. Nestled snugly around the silver handle, there's a lockbox, just like the attorney said. I spin the number combination and retrieve the gold-colored key from the box, turning it over in my hands a few times, wondering if this was the same key my uncle used. My hands tremble slightly as I place the key into the lock and push the door open wide.

Chapter 2

My breath catches in my throat. The cabin's interior is stunning—nothing like the way I remembered from my childhood. Though Uncle Dex was using it as a rental property, which I suppose explains all the fancy upgrades. After kicking off my boots by the heating vent to dry, I crank up the thermostat. The circular display reads sixty-five degrees. *That's not warm enough for a blizzard.* I tap the digital display until it reads seventy-two, and head off to explore.

The first room I find is the kitchen, and it's swankier than anything I've ever seen—crisp white-and-gray marble countertops, sleek dark cupboards, and a huge island lined with modern stools. Last but not least, the oven—a professional-grade dream with a gleaming metal hood. Oh my fucking god. This has to be a hallucination. There's no way this kitchen is real. Maybe *I could live here forever.* It's not an entirely impossible thought. I work remotely. I could stay here and rent the house out when I need extra income, just like uncle Dex did. This is exactly what I needed. Clarity, time away, and a space to figure out my next move. I've only been inside a few minutes and I've brainstormed two options. Sure, only one is realistic, but I'm making progress. Isn't that what my therapist said I needed to do in order to progress in my sessions with her? It doesn't matter. If I go with the second option—stay here forever—I could always replace my therapist if my case is proving 'too difficult.' *Maybe I don't need her after all. It's already working.* The giant tangled mess my brain has become is beginning to unravel and sort things out. *Best decision ever.* When was the last time I actually put my needs first? I can't even remember.

I shiver, shaking free from my thoughts, and trail my fingers along the wall in search of a light switch. Once they brush over the smooth cold plastic and flip them on, revealing a large oversized living area. The first thing I notice is the stonework on the fireplace extending from floor-to-ceiling. It's been black-washed to create contrast against the creamy ultra-light gray, nearly white walls. This house looks like it's right out of a magazine or a movie set. My eyes trace the sleek lines of the modern chandelier hanging from the dark walnut beams overhead—everything here feels extravagant. Did Uncle Dex pick this out himself? He used to be a famous house designer before he passed away. My dad told me he negotiated a plot of land for himself from the investor as part of his payment for designing the homes on the mountain. I continue studying the space, scanning it for anything familiar. The color pallete makes the room feel luxurious and chic. It looks like something straight out of a design magazine. A giant knit, cream-colored blanket is tucked into a basket on the hearth, next to a neat pile of freshly cut wood and kindling, complete with a sprinkle of pine needles on the floor. I smile, remembering how many times I begged to use the wood-burning fireplace in the summer. The old worn leather couches are long gone, replaced by a large cream-colored sectional the shade of a latte. Meticulously, my eyes continue to sweep the room in search of familiar sights. They wander up and down the walls, each time turning up empty-handed. It's like the entire cabin is a blank slate. Even the once golden pine planks have been replaced with dark walnut-stained exposed beams, transforming the room into a space that feels completely new.

I shiver again, wrapping my arms around myself, suddenly feeling completely out of place here. *Everything has changed.* The cabin walls feel like they are swallowing me alive. Panic attack. *Breathe. Close your eyes, and breathe. Why the fuck am I panicking? Because all of this is mine now and it's too good to be true. I don't think I deserve it.* I chastise myself, shaking my head as I try to slow my racing heart. I focus on a breathing exercise, inhaling deeply and counting the seconds, then exhaling until the tight grip of panic loosens. *It's late,* I remind myself. There will be plenty of time to spend exploring, time to figure out how I feel about this place. *For now,* I think, *I should probably get the car pulled into the garage and grab a few hours of sleep.* Stepping through the living room, the plush carpet squishes against my feet as I return to the oversized foyer to retrieve my boots. I notice how out of place they seem, kicked off next to the heating vent in haste. Given how hard the snow was falling, I should have pulled the car in right away. Sliding my boots back on, the panic from earlier is now replaced by determination. *It's going to be fine. I'll get things sorted out in the morning.* I shake the uneasiness from my mind as I pull the car in for the night.

Inside, the two-story, three-car garage is empty aside from a few of the usual tools. Against the wall, several snow shovels rest, waiting to be called to service. I eye them wearily, certain I will find myself in need of their assistance come morning. I slip the garage door opener from my pocket—thankfully, I remembered to grab it out of my purse when I got out of the car. *But* oops, *I left my purse in the car. Yet another reminder of why I need this vacation so badly.* I press the button and watch as the door glides open to reveal my car. The snow has covered it in a new layer of soft powder. I should have done this before exploring. It's even colder than I remember it being when I first walked inside. I absolutely do not want to brave the cold, but I have to. If I don't, I'm certain I'll be stuck digging my car out in the morning. Shit. I should have checked the fridge. I paid extra to have it stocked. *What if they couldn't make it out here because of the weather?* Will I be able to get to the grocery store if I need to? Fuck. My mind races as I pace back and forth between the car and the door, back to the fridge, unsure of what to do. A full ADHD spiral has commenced.

Then something catches my eye—movement in the tree line. My heart skips and immediately, I'm out of the throes of my indecisive loop. I freeze, my blood turning to ice. The snow swirls around me, and all I can see is the endless white haze. I squint through it, my eyes searching for whatever thought I saw. *Nothing. Nothing but dark, empty night.* My hands tremble as I press the unlock button. When the headlights flash on, I scan my surroundings as quickly as possible and bolt to the car. As soon as my ass slides across the cold leather, my hands reach out to slam the door closed and lock it. There's a can of mace In the glove compartment. I fumble for it, my fingers trembling as I grab it. Once the can is in my grasp, I exhale a shaky breath, feeling a little safer. But only a little. I turn the key but the engine's cold. *Of course, it's fucking cold.* And, for some reason, all I can think about is Tyler flipping the fuck out on me if I so much as thought about driving it in its current state. I press the door lock again, the action more for comfort than anything. Sitting there for a second, I try to calm my racing heart and shaking body. But then I see it again—movement in the trees. My body tenses and I'm frozen in panic once again. *Fuck warming up the engine.* I slam the shifter into gear and press the gas. Despite my rushed reaction, the car glides smoothly into the safety of the garage. I pull it through at an angle, parking more horizontally so I can simply complete my U-turn when I'm ready to leave later. Terrified when it looks like a shadow is moving outside, I click the garage door button and carefully watch the door close all the way before I get out of the car.

I collect my luggage from the back seat and rush back inside the cabin, heart sill pounding from the cold and lingering dread. It only takes me two trips to get everything inside, and as soon as I drop the second load onto the entryway floor, I lock the door behind me. I rush to check the front door lock, turning the deadbolt over to secure it. Leaving my luggage in the entryway, I slip off my boots again, then snag my overnight bag and head across the spacious living room to check the back doors are locked. My heart is pounding. I no longer care to slowly uncover every room in the house. I set my bag down on the sectional, but I don't let myself rest. I run from room to room with my mace, ready to defend myself against an intruder. I check the latches on the windows and every lock on the exterior doors. Content with my findings—all windows and doors secure—I collapse onto the sectional, my knees instinctively pulling in. I sit there, tense and completely on edge, for what feels like an eternity—until I finally convince myself to grab the blanket and settle in on the couch. On the sofa table, there's a remote. I grab it, almost frantically, and flip on the TV while retreating back to my safe spot on the couch and snuggle in for a cheesy holiday romance. The same kind I love to watch with my mom. I might be twenty-five years old, but I still love making cookies and watching holiday romcoms with my mom every year. A pang of guilt hits me just then. *I should have invited my parents.* After the breakup with Tyler, maybe it would have been better to have someone to lean on. But I wanted to do this on my own. I needed to process everything without anyone hovering over me. Still, I text her a long apology, explaining how sorry I am for not inviting them. But I don't send it right away. I want to re-read it in the morning, and I also don't want her to worry with me sending a message out so late. My eyes are getting heavy, and the movie is almost over, but the shadows in the unfamiliar space taunt and torment me. It feels like I'm ten years old all over again, except this time I'm not terrified to leave the safety of the couch for the bathroom. Instead, I'm terrified of what might be lurking in the shadows—or who. My heart beats faster as my mind wanders deeper into my thoughts. *What if it's the creepy cop from the exit?* Of course, my imagination runs wild with all kinds of different scenarios. The fear claws at me, and I'm exhausted. Soon I'm plunged into sleep, trapped inside of a nightmare I am responsible for dreaming up. My body may give in, but my mind doesn't.

Kane

Chapter 3

Silence surrounds me. The lake and wooded forest encircling its icy shores are quiet. The streets and trails are empty too. I squeeze the gas. *Correction: the forest was a deafening silence until the growl of my engine disturbed it.* My eyes sweep over the mountain. It's lifeless as I barrel my Polaris through the blowing snow. It comes in handy for everything. I smirk. *All that power rumbling to life can really turn a guy on.* My beast of a ride blasts through the powdery banks effortlessly, snow swirling heavy and thick, sticking to my all-black helmet as if Mother Nature is trying to warn my sweet little candy cane of my arrival—and the danger she's about to be in. *How dare you fucking try to warn her?* I think, pressing the gas, feeling threatened by a damn snow storm. I scoff. It doesn't matter. All that matters is that she's here. Hazel is really fucking here—on my mountain, with me. She doesn't know it yet, but she's all mine. Her body, her heart, maybe even her soul. I lick my lips just thinking about it. She's the one that got away, and I still can't believe this is happening. Everything about tonight has always felt too good to be true, from the moment her sweet, airy voice agreed to my demands to establish residency in exchange for the property. Sure, I may have impersonated an attorney and broken a few minor—okay, major—laws, but tomato, tomato, am I right? Honestly, I didn't expect for it to be so easy to lure her up here for a week alone with me. *Was there any harm really done?* On top of agreeing so easily, I also never expected for her to settle on the week of Christmas. Is she really that distraught over finding out about that other woman I set Tyler up with? What kind of depressed, lonely girl am I falling for? The grin on my face is pure satisfaction as I revel in the success of stage one of my plan.

It was easy enough to trick her into thinking I was a local police officer just doing my job when, in reality, I printed a magnetic sticker to impersonate a police vehicle and threw some lights on top of my truck. I even went so far as to order a custom-made police uniform under the guise that it was a costume for the local theater. By intercepting her at the bottom of the mountain, I was able to ensure she made it to her uncle's property safely. As soon as she turned down his road, I raced through the blizzard back to my house to grab the Polaris for an up-close look at Hazel. My body trembles with desire just thinking about running my hands over her supple skin. *Well, Kane, I think you just proved every woman who has ever said shoulders aren't sexy wrong.* Men just sexualize a woman's body, right? I roll my eyes at myself. I sure can't wait to study Hazel and sexualize her body. Despite the freezing cold temperatures, my dick still stiffens against my leg. *I know, buddy, soon enough...* Soon enough we'll get another glimpse at that slice of sunshine, all grown up.

When she rolled down her window for me earlier, it took every ounce of self-control to stop myself from taking her right then and there. All I could think about was slamming my lips against hers. For a brief moment, I considered doing it, but then the thrill of the chase wouldn't be nearly as much fun. I have all kinds of plans for the two of us this week. It's all going to be perfect. I just know it.

The soft glow from the lights I turned on at her new place earlier illuminates my path. Without them to guide my way, it would be much more difficult to see where I'm headed. The glow from the cabin is like a beacon leading me to a once-in-a-lifetime opportunity. At last, I have the chance to claim what is rightfully mine. *I saw her first.* I loved her first, and then she was ripped away from me, vanishing without a single trace.

My efforts to befriend her uncle were futile, but I didn't learn that until after the family feud was well underway. When Dexter's wife passed away tragically in a boating accident, let's just say I did him a favor. He deserved better than her. I needed something to spark a family reconciliation, and she proved to be the perfect sacrifice. Although I would have done anything to get Hazel back up this mountain. My efforts wouldn't have stopped there. It was a good thing her unexpected death worked like a charm. I weaseled my way in deeper with Dex, bonding over the loss of someone in a tragic boating accident. My mother murdered my father in cold blood, and I stood by watching, doing nothing to stop her. Together, we covered everything up. His life insurance policy paid off the mountain mansion, along with several other properties in his expansive portfolio, setting us up for life. We cashed in millions, and his investments continue to churn out revenue.

Mom has long since passed on. Cancer got her, so it was ironic that the day Dex found out he was terminal, I was the first person he told. I'd be lying if I said it didn't stir up buried emotions, but it also provided me with one last shot at getting Hazel home to me. I convinced him to leave his niece the rental property a few days later, and the will was amended immediately. He ended up leaving everything to her. I bet that really pissed her dad off. All those years of fighting over their father's estate, only for him to hand over his portion untouched to his only niece. When he passed, and she found out about her inheritance, I thought surely she would come and visit the place one last time before Dex passed away, but she never did. Not until now, and even then, she had to be lured up here. *Why is she so resistant,* I wonder, as if I haven't contemplated this very question thousands of times over the past few months?

When I get to the edge of her property line, I slow the Polaris and cut the engine, pocket my keys, then jump off in one fluid motion. The snow rises midway up to my shin as I sink into its ice-cold embrace. There's got to be at least 8 inches out here. I pop my helmet off, hang it from my handlebars and adjust the black subzero ski mask, re-situating it over my face from where it slid up. I check to make sure my tracker tag is securely attached to the ATV and my helmet, just in case. Most people up here know better than to mess with my stuff or trespass on my property, but sometimes people make bad choices. *And when they do, it's always fun to remind them of their place,* I snicker silently. Although I know the area like the back of my hand, the tracker will come in handy if the weather and visibility get worse. From the looks of the intensity of this storm, it very well could.

The trail system surrounding the lake stretches along my entire property, making it easy to get around on just the Polaris—much faster than driving the winding road from the top to the bottom. Hazel's newly inherited property just happens to be at the highest point, backing right up against my sprawling property line. I've acquired so many properties on the mountainside I own nearly half the mountain. *More luck.* Every time a property comes up for sale, I purchase it. Eventually, I plan to own the entire mountain. *Unless my darling Hazel would like to keep her uncle's gift.* It's the perfect wedding gift—paying off the taxes on her inheritance and allowing her to keep it, so long as she agrees to an eternity by my side. Satisfied with my brilliant idea, I check one last time to make sure my gear is on the up and up, then trek across her property, using the sprawling back deck as my guide. All those years tracking and hacking for the government really paid off, and when they fired me for failing my psych evaluation—well, they made me that much more valuable to the criminal sector. Taking care of Mom was always important to me and so, at the age of fourteen, we worked together to outsmart the system. I taught myself everything I could. I did a good job, too. The judge said I had, "a natural talent." I got busted by the feds when I was eighteen, just after graduation. *Mom always thought they were just waiting for the perfect opportunity to get me.* They ended up giving me the option of federal prison time or a full-ride scholarship to MIT with an agreement to work for them immediately following my graduation in order to pay off their investment in my education. I didn't need their money because I was a millionaire by then, and they had no idea I had enough money stashed in offshore accounts to buy my own private island if I wanted to. Let's just say the thought has crossed my mind many times. I'm still not convinced that I won't at some point before I die. At least not if I have my way. I shake my thoughts from my head again. It's important that I have a clear mind before I get close to her. I'm not sure I can trust myself to be this close again without touching her. I scan my surroundings one more time. In the distance, I can still make out the shoreline.

Beneath the glow of moonlight, the ice has formed layers on the lake, and it gleams like glass candy. By now, it should be most of the way frozen over for winter. Even the center of the lake should have a thin layer of ice over the surface. A gust of wind blows over the open space between the house and the tree line, sending me falling forward into the snow. *Damn, it's getting nasty out here.* I probably should head up the mountain, but my temptation drives my every move as I make my way, step by step, through the deep snow. I don't stop until it thins out beneath the deck. Huffing, I catch my breath. I'm incredibly fit. I work out every day, run a few local marathons, you know, the usual. Completely normal Colorado mountain millionaire behavior. So why does trekking through snow kick my ass every time? Maybe because it's so damn heavy? This is the good snow. It's perfect for snowballs, snowmen, building igloos, sledding—thank you density—and of course, snow ice cream. Yeah, I know that the last one is kind of a cheat, because all snow is good for snow ice cream. Great, now I'm just standing out here in the freezing cold thinking about ice cream. Earth to Kane, time to focus. We've got stalking to do. Curiosity gets the best of me and I maneuver my way around the perimeter until I arrive at the front of her house. Interesting. Her car is parked in the driveway. I hope she doesn't leave it there. I really don't want to shovel it out tomorrow when I show up to give her a warm welcome to the mountain.

The garage door groans as it creaks open. *Fuck.* I plaster myself against the side of the house. I'm out in the open. If I don't move, she's going to catch me. We can't have that. *On the plus side, at least I won't have to shovel her out.* I think as my eyes dart around the swirling snow. A few feet away, I spot a snow-covered bush. Time to make like a deer and run. Darting across the snow, I move as quickly as I can, which still feels like slow motion. Each time I kerflop into a deep spot, it takes forever to get my momentum going again. My run takes far longer than I would like and I end up diving face-first into the ice-cold snow just in time to avoid being spotted. The freezing cold flakes melt in my mouth. Oh, how I wish it was her sweet pussy melting in my mouth instead. Or ice cream. I would also rather be eating snow ice cream. Trying hard to laugh quietly, I peek out slowly from the cover of the bush, searching for her. I need to see Hazel, but the snow is so heavy it's impossible. There has to be a way to see that angelic face. After all these years, I've never met another woman as beautiful as her.

Our love story is expertly woven from when I first caught sight of her. I was twelve just shy of thirteen and my dad had just acquired the mountain property in Colorado. We were vacationing for the summer while he did some work in Denver on and off. Hazel told me she was twelve when we were playing Marco Polo in the lake's swimming section, but I found out later she was actually only eleven. We spent the entire summer together—and the one after, when I begged my father to take us back to the mountains. That was the summer my father had his accident. Hazel was long gone by then. I'd wanted her to be there, wished she could be—but instead, I was all alone. I think that's what triggered me to start losing my humanity. Or maybe it just contributed to an inevitable loss years later. *I'd ask my therapist, but she's dead.*

Absorbed in my thoughts, I wait patiently—despite the freezing temperature and blowing snow—for Hazel to pull the car into the garage and shut it. Then I dash around to the back to the stairs taking them two at a time. I creep along the patio until I am peering into the empty kitchen through the glass in the French doors. She's flipping on lights and walking around. As much as I want to stay and watch her, I can't risk being caught this early. I wait as long as I can, my stare lingering on her face, burning the image of her into every fiber of my memory. She's so fucking beautiful. Her ashy-blonde hair falls in loose waves over her shoulders. It's hard to believe standing only a few feet away is the gorgeous woman of my dreams.

Goddamn it. Hazel's beauty holds me captivated in place, as if she's put a fucking curse on me, forcing me to remain in place. I can't force myself to look away. Not when she's finally within my reach, so incredibly close to becoming mine to keep this Christmas. *Look away, you greedy fucking psycho. Get out of here.* I force myself to deny my innermost desires. It's some kind of fucking torture. Painfully aware that I only have a few more seconds to get away or further risk being caught, I hang my head in defeat, ordering myself to walk back to the Polaris before I ruin everything. *She'll still be here tomorrow,* I remind myself. Well, fuck, then I guess tomorrow can't come fast enough.

The ride home is miserable. Unable to keep my thoughts tucked away, I allow my mind to wander back to Hazel. Tonight was perfect. This snow storm makes it even easier to carry out my plans. With stage one complete, it's only a matter of time until I'm balls-deep inside of her, making Hazel take every inch of me. A moan escapes my mouth, rolling across my lips, vibrating them in a satisfying release of tension. I'm more than turned on. I'm starved for Hazel. She's the temptation pulsing through my veins, begging me to turn this ATV around and go flying back to her place. *Focus.* I shake my head. It's impossible to see anything in the near whiteout conditions. Times like this make me thankful that I know the way since I just cruised over the snowy terrain by muscle memory. My mind is far from the drive, and of course, my brain picks now to realize it's running completely on autopilot. *Don't panic. Don't panic.* Fuck, I'm totally panicking. Now is not the time to be getting lost in my thoughts. I need to stay focused. I'll have plenty of time to watch her on my screens when I get home—and bonus, it'll be warm enough to whip my dick out while I'm doing it.

Kane

Chapter 4

A light gust of wind blows a few rogue snowflakes across the frosty pane of the windshield, as if promising a much stronger return. I glare at them. I will not tolerate having my plans ruined. Mother Nature better keep herself in check. My body is running on autopilot again today as my hands wrap around the cold shifter, putting my truck in drive. For now, there's no telling how much of a window there is, and the sooner I get ahead of the storm, the easier it is to maintain once the snow starts falling again. The eye of a blizzard can sometimes last hours depending on the size of it. This is exactly why I got up early. I have an entire mountainside to plow. In the distance, the sun threatens to attempt a morning appearance. So far, despite the effort, the sky remains an uncomfortable dark—overcast and gray—as the intensity builds for round two of our pounding. I can't help the ridiculous grin forming on my lips. The mountain isn't the only thing that's going to be getting a pounding this week. *Is it too soon to be thinking about that? Do I care if it's too soon?* I think long and hard about it, mulling things over. *Nope. And this is why the therapist said I'm a psychopath—or maybe she said I had psychopathic tendencies?* I shrug my shoulders. *It didn't matter once I realized it was her who wrote the recommendation to HR, giving them everything they needed to fire me. I made sure she learned an unfortunate lesson about what happens to dirty fucking snitches. Come to think of it, she was my first kill.* My cock strains against my jeans, suddenly awake. Fuck. Am I really turned on from just remembering that night? I guess whatever she said about me was right because here I am plowing my way down the mountain to succumb to my darkest desires while acting out my ultimate fantasy.

The drive down to Hazel isn't terrible. The truck slid a few times, but that's because the ATV in the truck bed makes it extra heavy. I pull up in front of the cabin, if you can even call it that, because all the cabins on the mountain are really just mansions made to look like giant oversized cabins and wood lodges. Time to mentally prepare myself, but the gorgeous architecture distracts me. Uncle Dex really knew what he was doing when he designed all of them. Not a single one is the same. Each one is completely unique, customized by their original purchasers. I take a moment to appreciate the stone work and sloping wood beams that frame the oversized front porch. I wonder if she even realizes, yet the property she inherited is worth millions. She's a lucky girl, I hope she knows that. I pull on my extra thick gloves. It's time to get to clearing the snow. I'm not a slumlord, after all. Normal people would probably contract out the work. It's not like I can't afford to. It's a choice. I find plowing the mountain soothing, and it gives me something better to do with my time.

The plow on the Polaris makes clearing the entire giant driveway easy. All the driveways up here are heated, too. Before I leave, I'll slip inside and turn on the timer to make things easier. Once I finish the driveway, I return to the truck to grab my shovel. I don't want to wake her with the snowblower. This morning is for me. It's an excuse to sneak inside and watch her. I crave companionship like my lungs crave air, and Hazel has always been the one. The fact that I've spent my entire adult life knowing she was made for me, that we were destined to meet as young children, to be one another's first crushes, and then end up together, speaks volumes. I'm borderline obsessive. *Another label from the dead doctor's notes.* While she's right about my obsessive, stalker-like tendencies, I'm not convinced my behavior is harmful if I care about the person I'm hyper-fixated with. No, I'm only fucking harmful when you've personally wronged me. *Just like Dex's wife.* That bitch thought she could blackmail me into not telling Dex about the little affair she was having. Fuck around and find out. I didn't have to tell him. I simply cleaned up the mess by eliminating the person hurting him. Why'd I do it? I guess because Dex really was a good guy. He was a good friend and he deserved better.

After finishing the front, I bend over with my hands on my knees to catch my breath, and pull the ski mask from my face. I run my hand through my hair to calm my thoughts. This is exactly why I have to test myself. I'm not sure if I can trust the darker side of me to be around her. The urge to collect her is already nipping at the edge of my thoughts. If I can make Hazel fall in love with a monster like me, then maybe, just maybe, I can bring this holiday tradition to an end.

I toss the shovel over my shoulder and whistle a Christmas tune as I work my way along the service sidewalk that leads around to the back. Once I finish the steps leading up to the deck, I take the shovel back to my truck, tucking it away for later. I can't make trying to escape the house easier for her. *One way in, one way out.* From the passenger seat, I snatch the gift basket filled with muffins and gourmet coffee, along with a red gift bag full of specialty handmade soaps. They were crafted with care and an extra special ingredient—a trade my mother taught me. We used to bake and make soap together all the time, even after Dad's accident. I don't want to think about those memories now, though. Not when I'm turned on, knowing that later she'll be washing with my cum. The thought of it coating her body has my cock throbbing and straining against my pants. I imagine the suds running over her breasts and peaked nipples. My erection is so hard, it's painful. I set everything back down on the passenger seat. One hand reaches above me to steady myself against the door frame while the other unzips my pants, sliding inside to grip the base of my cock. My balls tighten in excitement. They know exactly what's about to happen. With my back to the house and the door of the truck blocking everything else, I work my hand firmly over my dick. As I do, I close my eyes, imagining Hazel in the shower again and the soap running over her breasts before cascading down to drip across the slit of her pussy. I use my thumb to rub the pre-cum leaking out over my swollen head, then spread it down my very erect shaft, allowing my made-up scene to continue playing out. The soap covers her hands in thick suds as she rubs it over and through her folds, working my spent cum all over that tight pussy. I can't wait to make her mine. *Fuck, I'm going to come.* I keep my rhythm, stroking myself over the edge, watching as the warm cum shoots from my dick, melting into the snow. Once I've pumped my dick dry, I return it to my pants, zipping them and no longer burdened with an insatiable need. It was probably best I got that out of my system before being so close to Hazel.

Recovered from my fantasy session, I grab the gifts and head up the front path as if it's just a normal day checking on the property. It's much lighter now as the sun works its way out, still fighting to burst through the thick, heavy snow clouds looming overhead. More neighbors—or vacationers, in the case of my multiple rental properties—could be awake and watching, so I move about casually and as quietly as can be, using my key to slip inside the cabin effortlessly. *Am I so desperate and insane that I'll risk everything just to get a closer look at her? Fuck yes, I am.* All those years of earning her uncle's trust have finally paid off full circle.

Inside the house, I am caught off guard when I round the hallway leading from the entryway to the kitchen and oversized, two-story living room. I did not expect to find her sleeping there, curled up beneath a warm blanket while a cheesy holiday romance movie plays in the background. I thought she glimpsed me last night. Hazel must have been too shaken up afterwards to sleep in the bedroom. Honestly, I can't blame her, but finding her here like this was an unneeded ego boost. Now I'm not sure if I should feel bad about the situation or be proud of myself. My cock twitches and I glare down at it for a moment. *Go to sleep. We do not need another session.* Fuck, I can't believe I'm talking to my crotch like this. How fucking embarrassing. It's a good thing Hazel is sleeping and no one else is around to see this. It's only been a few minutes alone together and I'm struggling to control myself.

I place the gifts on the kitchen island. A special treat for a special girl. I'll be back later to make sure she fully enjoys the basket. I want her to feel right at home here. A smile spreads across my lips as I slink back through the kitchen, slowly backing my way into the living room—forgetting she's on the couch—until I realize I'm standing so very fucking close to her. The warm, sweet notes of her vanilla, maybe coconut, shampoo taunt me, urging me to take another deep breath. I can smell more than just her shampoo. The lingering scent of perfume mixes with it, and fuck if she doesn't smell like goddamn temptation. A sweet, spicy, erotic scent tickles my nose. I love the way she smells. I can't get enough. Inhaling deeply, I savor the scent of her. *I'm already this close. I may as well get a closer look at my prize.*

She's so fucking beautiful, curled up beneath the giant knit blanket. Her hair falls in wisps across her rose-tinted cheeks, flushed from sleep. I can't help but stare—like the silent stalker I am. When she accepted the stipulation of staying up here to take possession of the cabin, I knew it was my one and only chance. The chance I spent years putting in the work building a relationship with her uncle for. A once- in-a-lifetime opportunity to make the first girl I ever loved mine. I've waited so long to claim Hazel; she should have been mine from the start. I waited, summer after summer, doing everything I could to forget about her, but I never did. No girl ever compared to her. It wasn't without effort either. I dated, I fucked, but it was always emotionless. They meant nothing to me. Unable to connect with women on an emotional level left me fucking for my pleasure and my pleasure alone. I became more and more dangerous, especially after my mother's death, and even more so after I made my first kill. It wasn't until then that I started enjoying women for sport—never appreciative of who they were—because I gave no fucks about them. There could only ever be two women worthy enough of my love—and one was already dead and gone. But Hazel, she's finally here. Right within my reach. What I wouldn't give to hold her in my arms, caressing her supple skin with my greedy fingers.

Hazel would be different. I need to promise to stay in control. Then when I take her—when I splay her tight pussy across my waiting cock—I'm going to feel satisfaction and emotional connection for the first time. I'm going to feel every fucking stretch and squeeze, as well as each and every emotion that I've ever denied myself. It's going to be so fucking goddamn glorious. And I am also hyper-aware of precisely how cautious I will need to be. The slightest fuck-up and my entire plan will be ruined. My hands ache to touch her, but I deny myself the gratification. It's not worth it for a few feels. It would only be a tease at a good time. For Hazel, everything has to be perfect. No mistakes. No rushing. No fucking impulsiveness.

My eyes drop to her plump pink lips, and my own let out a husky, needy sound. My dick flexing in response. I imagine they will feel like heaven once they are wrapped around my throbbing cock while I fuck her throat, until I spill every last drop of my cum into her. Satisfied, I smile at the thought of her choking on it, as I glide it through her tits, fucking them and her mouth at the same time. I'm nearly panting at my lucid thoughts, which leaves my cock aching and full of desire. As much as I want to stand here watching her sleep until she wakes up to stare into my eyes like a frightened little deer in headlights, it's time to go. The sun is making its presence known, threatening to spill in through the slats of the blinds. She'll wake up anytime, and when she does, the sooner she will discover the gifts I've left for her on the countertop. I can only guess how emotionally and physically exhausted Hazel is, so to help the process of waking her along, I stride over to the wall with the thermostat, then crank that sucker down to sixty degrees. The storm brought with it bitterly cold temperatures, meaning with the heat cranked down the oversized, open-concept mansion-cabin, will get chilly fast. Once again my imagination wanders off on me as I picture her waking up confused and groggy, her nipples peaked and hard beneath her shirt as she scrambles to the thermostat. I look toward the camera I planted earlier, calculating whether or not it will capture the scene I just played out. Before I leave, I adjust it ever so slightly, then slip back out the front door just as quietly as when I entered

The massive oak door closes softly behind me on my way out, turning the lock gently, then walking to my truck with a jaunty skip in my step. I can't wait for my little obsession to see what I've left for her. I whistle another Christmas-themed tune to myself before climbing inside and turning the truck around so I can plow the rest of the road leading down the mountain and into town. I have a few things I need to pick up for later, in anticipation of what's coming, and what I have planned for my sweet temptation. The cameras are on, ready to record, and waiting to alert me as soon as they sense movement. Hazel looked so peaceful laying there resting. I can't get over the sight of her. *In good time,* I remind myself.

Chapter 5

It's freezing cold when my eyes flutter open, and I shiver despite being swaddled beneath the warm, thick blanket. I blink a few times to clear the sleep from my eyes. For a moment, I forget where I am, looking around, confused, as I try to regain my senses. Eventually, it all comes crashing back to me in a heavy wave of emotions. I'm in the middle of the woods, during a blizzard, because I'm a stubborn woman, hell-bent on getting away from the reality of my breakup, and the recent death of my uncle. *Oh no, the storm. Don't panic until you look outside, Hazel.* What was I thinking coming up here last night? Tyler begged me not to come, but he should be the least of my worries. I never checked the pantry or the fridge last night. Even though I paid uncle Dex's rental property servicer extra to fully stock the kitchen, I have trust issues thanks to my asshole ex-boyfriend. Subconsciously, I pull my bottom lip beneath my teeth, chewing on it. *Anxiety is such a fucking bitch.* On the off chance I need food or something for survival, I wonder if the roads are even passable? I suppose I should leave the comfort of this incredible couch and warm blanket to not only investigate the conditions, but also the source of the cold. Luckily, Uncle Dex designed these houses with actual wood-burning fireplaces. If the electricity is out, at least I can stay warm curled up next to the fire. Groaning, I swing my feet off the couch and onto the cold carpet. A shiver runs through me. The heat has been off for a while if the floor is this cold. Wrapping the blanket around my shoulders, I stumble sleepily to the thermostat for inspection.

I don't make it all the way to the hallway, distracted by the sunshine gleaming in barely through the back French doors leading from the kitchen out onto the large oversized deck that spans the entire back of the house. Honestly, the deck is probably the same size, if not bigger, than my entire ground floor in the Denver townhouse. Curious as to how many inches cover the ground, I hurry to the door, changing course to peek outside at the drifts. My breath sucks in with a surprised whoosh. There must be at least two feet of snow out there. It presses itself against the glass panes, as if straining to burst through the glass and inside the insane luxury kitchen. The more I look around, the more I'm seriously considering selling the townhouse and moving in here forever. Ha—you wish, Hazel. *Never say never,* a small voice whispers in my head, but I ignore it.

Everywhere I look the sun rains down sparkles. It's like we're in a frosted wonderland. The view from the back is impressive. As far as I can see, even down to the shoreline of the lake, there's nothing but pristine, untouched snow. It covers the trees, dripping from them like melted white chocolate. There are no animal tracks, or footprints to be seen—just perfect undisturbed nature, and it's goddamn refreshing. If the view from here is this gorgeous, I wonder what it looks like from the top of the mountain, staring down at all the other snow-covered homes. I make a mental note to watch *Jack Frost* later—it's a classic, and I'm sure I can sign into all my apps and find it somewhere. I scurry off to the giant, winding staircase. As I creep up the perfectly undisturbed carpet, my footsteps are so quiet, it feels like I wouldn't even hear someone else moving around here. *Stop it, don't think like that. You're going to get all up in your head.* Fuck, too late. I'm definitely going to freak myself out. From the upstairs landing I stare out a giant window. I used to love coming up here to look at the stars, but today, it's snow that captures my gaze. All down the mountainside, the giant cabins are nestled beneath fluffy white peaks of frosting, like gingerbread homes just waiting to be decorated. It makes me smile—this was the moment I longed for as a child. Another shiver reminds me why I woke up to begin with. Back downstairs I go, on a mission to check the thermostat.

The thermostat reads sixty-two degrees. I stare at it in disbelief. I know I clicked it up to seventy-two last night. *Didn't I? Maybe I didn't.* I shrug, unsure of anything I remember from last night. It was so late, and I was exhausted by the time I arrived. There's no telling for sure what I dreamed, imagined, or what actually happened. But I can't forget the creepy cop—something was off about him. When he smiled, it didn't quite reach his eyes. Hopefully, I don't run into him again, ever. Sixty-two degrees, though—no wonder I am freezing. Maybe the thermostat is on some kind of auto cycle. I spend the better part of thirty minutes reprogramming the temperatures and times for my stay. It's going to take longer than I want before the house warms back up. My stomach rumbles as I pull the blanket tighter around my shoulders. I side-eye the pile of wood resting next to the fireplace and shrug. Food can wait. A childish grin spreads across my lips as I make my way back to the cozy living room and start building a fire. This is a childhood dream come true. As soon as the wood starts burning, I lean closer, inhaling deeply, taking in every last bit of the comforting smell. My dad and Uncle Dex taught me how to build fires, and the memory makes me feel a little closer to them both right now. Of course, I just miss Dad because I haven't seen him in over three months. Between work and the cruise he and Mom just took, we simply haven't had time to get together. He would like this. Uncle Dex would like this. Suddenly, I'm beaming and tears are streaming down my face. This trip and alone time are exactly what I needed. The smell of the fire fills the room. It smells like healing—like fond memories from my childhood. I tend the fire like an overprotective mother until it crackles and pops. Even the cool bricks of the hearth begin to warm beneath me. A second, more urgent grumble from my stomach disturbs the rhythm of the crackling wood. Satisfied with my fire-building skills, I brave a trip to the kitchen to scrounge up some food. *I really hope they fucking stocked the kitchen like I paid them to,* I think with a grimace.

To my surprise, when I walk into the kitchen, there's a basket and a red gift card perfectly positioned in the center of the gleaming marble island.

"That's strange," I whisper. "I don't remember seeing this last night."

Intrigued, I slide the basket across the counter to where I can get a better look at it. The basket is wrapped up all nice and neat in plastic cellophane, stuffed full of over-sized muffins in an array of varieties, including poppy-seed—yum. Behind the pile of muffins are small bags of flavored coffee. On the top, wrapped up in a bow, is a small white envelope with my name on it. I scan the kitchen for signs of a coffee maker, noticing a fairly fancy machine on the far counter, set up as a coffee bar. With its location acquired, I open the cupboards in search of sugar. To my surprise, I find them fully stocked full of anything I could possibly need. In the third cupboard, I find the sugar, flour, and other baking essentials. My search expands to the refrigerator, which I am pleased to see is fully stocked as well. I locate the half-and-half, snatching it up quickly from its shelf. My steps are filled with excitement, having found the ingredients necessary to conjure up some liquid gold. There's even a little carafe with different flavored syrups. It's a coffee lover's dream come true.

Before I get the fancy coffee brewing, I turn back to the gift basket, eyeing the ribbon holding everything in place. It's a really pretty package. I snap a picture in case I decide to post it on my social media. *Maybe it'll piss Tyler off.* It's petty of me, but it was petty of him to bring another girl into our home and fuck her in our bed. I mean, who the hell actually does something like that to their partner? I don't even want to think about it. Ugh. I snap the photo, then pull the tail of the bow, watching as everything unravels. It's oddly satisfying, and I only feel a little guilty as I untie the basket. The promise of hot caffeine rejuvenating my soul next to a crackling fire makes that guilt disappear fast.

I slide the crisp white envelope open and remove the card. Written neatly in black pen is a short welcome message for my stay, along with the property caretaker's phone number. His name is Kane. *I wonder if Kane is cute. Suddenly remembering my cheesy Christmas romance movie fantasy.* I stuff the card back in the envelope and place it next to the basket. Once the coffee finishes brewing, I grab a small plate from the cupboard and carry my coffee and a poppyseed muffin over to the hearth. The muffin is moist and savory—easy to devour between sips of coffee.

When I finish, I place another log into the fire to keep it burning and head back for seconds. I may as well enjoy myself. I no longer have Tyler's voice in my head, taunting me for indulging, or accusing me of overeating. I will never have to hear him make hurtful comments about my body again. It feels so fucking gratifying. Freedom pulses through my veins, and it feels like everything I dreamed it would be. I waddle my cute muffin booty back to the warmth of the fireplace, setting my mug and plate on the end table, then snag my phone from the couch, which hasn't stopped flashing since I woke up. I don't want to talk to Tyler or my parents—they mean well, but I just want to lose myself in my thoughts right now. I want to retreat, to breathe, to do whatever I want, whenever I want, even if that means doing absolutely nothing at all. This is the fresh start I've needed—the beginning of a season of me. Popping bites of blueberry muffin in my mouth, I scroll through the notifications. *The blueberry is just as good as poppyseed. I can't wait to try the cinnamon crumble next.* I skim the messages, and twenty messages are from Tyler alone. I don't bother opening them—I can tell from the text preview that they're all cringy and clingy. He's clearly hit the point where he thinks he can crawl back and I'll take him, just like all the other times. Not this time. I deserve better. My eyes glaze over a line that says if he has to fly out here to bring me back, he will. I scoff so hard that I snort, barely containing the coffee from shooting out of my nose.. When I finally swallow, I'm cackling like a hyena. If anyone could hear me right now, they might actually think I've gone completely off the deep end.

The laughter eventually tapers off as I continue to check my messages. My mom's message surprises me. It's short and not even prying, like she's actually giving me some of the space I need to heal on this trip. There's one from Lexie checking on me, so I send one back, letting her know I am here and settled, then switch my phone to silent and flip on another cheesy holiday romance movie. I'll get to Jack Frost later. I'm such a sucker for these movies. They're the perfect escape from my own life, and they give me hope that maybe one day I will meet *the one*. I think about the mysterious caretaker, Kane, and hope he's bearded and hunky—though I would settle for abs and a cute face. Grinning from ear to ear, I snuggle back into the same spot I slept in, feeling only a small amount of guilt for squandering my time curled up on this couch for the entire stay. I have all week. What's a few more hours? It's still way too cold to venture out of this room, so I promise myself I'll go exploring and get properly settled into a bedroom after this movie, but until then I am fully immersing myself in the romance.

I'm not sure if it's because of the emotional exhaustion, the warmth of the fire, or my full belly, but my eyelids are growing heavy. It's becoming quite clear there's no amount of caffeine that can save me from the food coma I am about to enter. My body feels heavy as every muscle slowly relaxes, melting me into the soft cushions of the sectional. At first I imagine what it might be like if my life were like one of those movies. This is my shot. This trip is my opportunity to live out a holiday meet-cute and be swept off my feet by a handsome Prince Charming. I fall asleep, blissfully dreaming about my perfect holiday romance story. I can't wait to drive down to the town so I can bump into the man of my dreams. As I slumber away for who knows how long, in a deep restorative sleep, where my own movie is playing out scene by scene.

Chapter 6

After a solid hour spent plowing the main road down the mountain, then another heading into town and back for supplies, I'm finally pulling both the truck and the Polaris into the garage. Once I finish unloading the Polaris, I crank the garage heater on and turn on the heated floor. I need everything dry and ready to go at a moment's notice once my tempting little morsel of Christmas fantasies falls victim to her muffin-induced slumber. Did I lace those muffins with something to help Hazel sleep? I sure did. In the mudroom, I set down the grocery bags then slip off my snow boots and shrug out of my layers. The anticipation of tuning in to watch Hazel all day is overwhelming my focus. I've waited years to be this close to her again. On my way to the kitchen for a snack, I peek into my office at the myriad of screens all set up with different tiled views of Hazel's newly-inherited house. My eyes sweep over every square, scanning each one for signs of movement. Nothing yet. She's still right where I left her. This gives me the perfect opportunity to slip away to warm up cocoa while I wait on my oh-so-tempting-treat to wake up. In the kitchen, I warm up an extra large Christmas mug full of milk, stirring in the powder mixture of my peppermint hot chocolate with a miniature candy cane. I hang the candy cane from the edge of the cup and take a sip.

"Mmmm, so good," I groan as I return to my office for some screen time. Once I've settled into my chair comfortably, I pull up the camera feeds that give me a clear view of Hazel, then isolate them into a repetitive loop stream. I move the window to one of my available monitor screens, letting the stream of her take over the entire screen.

"Don't worry, little doe, I'm watching. Sleep as long as you need." I say to the computer screen, my tone much raspier and filled with need than I intended.

I've always wondered what it would be like to wake up next to her and, for now, this is the closest I'll get. Leaning back, I allow the plush leather chair to wrap me in its embrace, taking another swig of cocoa. My eyes drift back to the screen where Hazel sleeps peacefully, and a long sigh escapes me. She moves, moaning softly in her sleep. It sets off my notifications, but I ignore them, too transfixed on the way my dick responded to her sleep-induced moan. My girl is finally waking up and I'm ready to spend the next few hours watching her every move. So long as the weather continues to work in my favor, because if the snowband bulks up as predicted, we may end up snowed in on the mountain. What a shame it would be if we ended up trapped together over the Christmas holiday. Christmas Eve is only a few days away.

The camera alarm sounds again, interrupting my thoughts and alerting me to movement. I'm happy to see the house is as cold as I hoped. The first thing Hazel does is sit up and shiver, her nipples instantly pebbling against her shirt. It's fucking adorable the way she looks around, confused by the sudden cold. I can tell by the scowl on her face she's not excited to investigate her chilly awakening.

Hazel's feet swing over the edge of the couch and onto the carpet. I watch as she pulls the blanket around her. The white cotton shirt is making it easy for me to see her perfect tits bouncing beneath them as she trudges around the house. My hand slides against the band of my long underwear to grasp my hard cock. I'm so fucking turned on just watching her. She fumbles around the cabin, completely forgetting all about the thermostat. My greedy hand slides down my hard length once then back up again, until I'm stroking my dick from base to tip rhythmically. I'm more worked up than I intended to be. Either I finish the job here alone, or I take a few deep breaths and regain my composure. *Decisions, decisions,* I think to myself, loosening my grip and ripping my eyes away from the screen. *Why does she have to be so goddamn sexy?* I stare up at the ceiling for a minute and inhale deeply before I squeeze my eyes shut and focus on calm, steady breathing. *Fuck. Think unhappy thoughts, come on.* I giggle. *Cum on.* I'm ridiculous. It's working though. I try to think about Tyler. No way can I think about him and still be turned on. I pull up some of the background programming I built to keep tabs on him. A quick glance shows me his card transactions, phone calls, and the tracker on his car is logging locations. This attracts more of my attention and I'm suddenly engrossed in studying everything he's done in the last twenty-four hours. If I didn't know any better, I would suspect he's planning to come after her. That can't happen. It *won't* happen. Hazel belongs with me. Suspicious, I pull up his airline ticket information by extracting his login and signing into his account. He has an active one-way ticket flying into Aspen, Colorado. I'll definitely be monitoring his emails to watch for a cancellation. *What are you up to, Tyler?* My jaw twitches from the way I'm angrily clenching it. I'll have to check on him later—I wasn't planning on having to take him out. I thought the money and replacement girlfriend were a good deal and when we struck our bargain, so did he.

Now that I'm back in control, it's time to check in on my girl. *My girl.* It has such a nice ring to it. I click around, returning to my multi-camera view, delighted to see she's building herself a fire. There's a camera mounted to the beams above her, giving me an all-access view down her cleavage. Once the fire is crackling, Hazel wanders into the kitchen. *Please eat the muffins. Please, please, please.* I silently pray.

Hazel examines the basket of muffins. I'm instantly on edge and antsy, waiting to see if she eats one. My entire focus is on the screen, on pins and needles, waiting to watch this dubious part of my plan play out. She opens the bag, reading the card. Oh sweet victory, she's pulling out a muffin and placing it on a plate. I'm damn-near fucking giddy watching as she devours it. As soon as she finishes, I glance at my watch, noting the time, then start the stopwatch on my phone. The moment the drugs enter her system, I'll only have so much time. The fake menus for local restaurants are already prepped and packed in a plastic bag, ready to come with me. Hazel's going to be hungry after such a long nap. Lucky for her, I'll be close by to deliver whatever her heart desires.

My attention returns to the screen to watch and wait for the drugs to take effect. There's no sense in rushing to get ready. This is a simple test run to see how long she stays incapacitated. It's like a bonus round to scare her, just enough to keep her on edge and cop a feel. Leaving without touching her earlier this morning was torture, es-pecially when she was within arm's reach—tempting and vulnerable, just waiting to be mine for the taking.

"Calm down, Kane," I remind myself in a whisper.

I'm not sure what or who I am trying to hide from. I live alone up here at the peak of the mountain in a large mansion. It's way too big for one person, but that's what's so great about this entire situation. If all goes as planned, it can be me and Hazel together forever, with all the time in the world to spend together. She will never have to go back to work. My investments have been good to me. I make so much passive income that I'll never have to work an actual day the rest of my life. Even if I did suddenly need money, I have all my connections. I can find work easily.

Shit! She's eating a second muffin. I want to talk to her through the screen and tell her to stop—that she'll ruin the perfect day I had planned for the two of us—but I don't need her to know I'm watching her, not yet. My keyboard goes flying across the room, smashing onto the floor and breaking into several pieces as the keys pop off. This isn't ideal, I want her to stay alive. I'm trying really hard to control myself. Now I'm going to have to spend the better part of my day trapped in the same room as her, monitoring her. It shouldn't be enough to overdose, but I won't be taking chances where she is concerned. I guess I won't mind being inside the house all alone, just the two of us. I practically moan as my dick strains against my pants, reminding me just how badly I want her—how badly I've always wanted her. It doesn't matter. None of it matters. The only thing that matters is that she's here now and waiting for me. I watch her on the screen eagerly, continuing to get lost in my own thoughts as I wait for her to fall asleep. A little over thirty minutes later, she drops off, the Christmas movie playing in the background. It's my cue to head out the door and back down the mountain to pay my sweet obsession a visit.

Kane

Chapter 7

The keys to Hazel's front door clang in the cupholder as the truck bounces down the curving dirt road, leading from the back of my property to the lake along the edge of hers, where a connecting easement spits drivers back onto the main road. The storm is picking up again, and there's at least three inches of fresh snow. I bet we get at least another foot by the end of tonight, but I'll be damned if I'm going to let that stop me from spending time with Hazel. My tires skid over a slick spot and the truck slides around a curve in the road. Snowflakes dance around the windows of the truck, swirling as if trying to fight me off, but there's nothing that can keep me away from my temptation. Instinctively, I lower the plow and let it run as I drive. Nothing about hiking home in a blizzard sounds fun to me. It's much easier to keep this part of the road clear. The town plow can worry about the rest of the road for all I care, and I won't be disappointed if he can't make it out this way for several more hours... or maybe even days. The snow crunches beneath my tires loudly, as if trying to warn Hazel I've arrived. Before I get out of the truck, I swipe open my phone and check the cameras. She's still asleep. *Good.* It hasn't been long enough for all that Ambien to wear off. I shut the truck off. Time to act normal. I've got to sell it so that if anyone notices me shoveling in the middle of the day, they won't think twice to question why I am here. Nonchalantly, I step out of the truck and my boots plummet into the powdery fresh snow. My breath hangs in the frosty air as I stomp over the snow to grab a shovel from the back of the truck. Then I set to work, clearing myself a path to the door. If she wakes up in time to see things are shoveled, I'm sure she'll just assume it's the property management company without further suspicion.

Once I've made it to the front porch, I lean the snow shovel against the side of the house and check the cameras. *Still sleeping.* I glance at my stopwatch timer, mentally setting a time limit of an hour until it's safe, then I can retreat up the mountain and wait for her to call for delivery. *Oh, what fun it's going to be tonight.* I turn the key in the door for a second time and step inside. It's warm again. I leave the thermostat alone and side-eye the dying fire. Before I do anything, I head to the garage to disconnect her battery terminal. There's a screwdriver in one of the shop cupboards at the back of the third bay. I retrieve it and breathe a sigh of relief when I find she's left the car unlocked. This is going to be easier than I thought. I release the hood, then slide out to pop the terminal off. I arrange it so, without inspection, it appears to be in place. Perfect. *What will she do when she realizes her car won't start?* A maniacal grin spreads across my lips as I put the screwdriver away and return to the warm house.

The first thing I do inside is slip off my boots on the entry rug before stepping onto the carpet. No need to leave any evidence that I'm here. I think about carrying them with me, but instead decide that I will leave before she wakes up. Stealthily, I creep my way across the soft plush carpet to the fireplace. The fire is dying down, so I place another couple of logs on it to keep the flames burning. She looked so happy building it—who am I to take that from her? I'd much rather take her lying next to it. My dick agrees, blood rushing to it as I engross myself in a momentary fantasy. Once it's done playing in my head, I finish out the task. I would hate for her to catch a cold. Who am I kidding? That's a lie. I would love to watch those perky tits bounce around, nipples hard all over again as she coughs from sickness. I stare at her, imagining she's riding my cock with her tits bouncing in my face for a few minutes, then shake my head and get down to business. *Get it together. Stop getting lost in your thoughts.*

Pulling my attention away from her is hard, but I have several tasks I'm hoping to accomplish. It's so hard to leave her when all I want to do is sit down and watch her. I check my settings, making sure all my alerts are on. Humming a Christmas tune, I pop one earbud in my ear so I can listen for alerts and leave the other ear to listen to the sound of silence inside the sprawling cabin. I return to the entryway where her luggage lays hastily abandoned, likely from her little scare of catching my shadowy outline last night. *I had a feeling she saw me.* The least I can do is help her unpack. I stack a few pieces on her suitcase plus grab another duffle bag, looping it over my shoulder, and rolling it all down the hallway to the main bedroom.

The room itself is gorgeous. Her uncle spared no expense when he was renovating this place. I should know I helped him do everything. We talked often about how he didn't just want it to be an easy income generator, but part of him hoped he could win her over with this one last attempt. I think he secretly hoped she would either decide to live up here, or at the very least come back year after year, the way he always dreamed she would one day. It's sad how hard he tried to mend their relationship, and she dug her heels in resisting every attempt. I hated her for it at first, but when he showed me the will and explained he finally left the cabin to her, I let those feelings go. I knew some way, somehow, I could lure her up here—right into my dangerous arms. People don't always make good decisions when they are hurting, and I intended to capitalize on all of Hazel's pain for my own gain. I make a second trip back for the rest of her stuff, carrying it effortlessly. I grab the first suitcase, fling it onto the bed with a plop and unzip it. Her clothes are neatly folded and organized. They smell of fresh laundry detergent. I pull out a T-shirt, running my fingers over it, inhaling the smell of her. One by one, I moved each item out of her suitcase and into the drawers, emptying all her luggage and stacking it nicely next to the closet door. I saved her panties for last. They lay in a pile on her bed, waiting for me. I drop all but the last pair in, choosing to slip the lacy black material into my pocket, then slide the drawer closed. Next, I walk into the bathroom, checking to make sure the additional special soaps I made for her, candles, and towels are how I left them when I set everything up. I even stocked the shower full of several shampoos and conditioners, and took the liberty of filling them with an extra special ingredient: Cand a la Kane. My girl is going to bathe in my cum. Before I leave, I check the camera placements on my phone app and hurry back to Hazel. Everything on my to-do list today is complete and I've been dying to touch her—I need to know she's real.

The cameras on my phone show her right where I left her snoozing away in her Ambien-laced slumber. In the living room, I lean over the back of the couch, admiring the shape of her. Her ashy-blonde hair is strewn across her face, scraping it back gingerly. I tuck it behind one ear. My fingers reach around her ear, then trace her jawline tenderly. I run the back of my hand across her shoulder and down her arm. She moves into my touch, groaning softly as if she's aroused. I do it a second time, but on the next pass, I drape my fingers down to her hipbone. She moans again in her sleep and I suck my breath in, trying not to pant. *Dare I take another pass?* When I tested the dosing on myself, I was out for about four hours. I check my master timer, which tells me it's been five hours. My second timer shows it's been two hours. Time flies when you're having fun, I guess. My time is up, but I'm not ready to go. *One more touch,* I decide, *and then I must depart.* I run my hand back up her body from her hip, slowly curving across her waist, then dipping a finger across her breast, swirling around her nipple one time, dragging it up her neck, and brushing my thumb across the swell of her bottom lip.

She moans, pulling my thumb in between her soft plump lips, giving my thumb a nibble. Oh my fuck. If there is a God, then I consider myself blessed. I bite the knuckle on my finger to keep from moaning. My cock wakes, ready and at attention. I glance down at her hard nipples and fuck, I'm about to throw the entire plan out the window. It's time to go but she's swirling her tongue across the tip of my thumb, and everything is getting hazy. My other hand loses control, making one more drag down her chest, cupping her breast as my thumb runs across her pebbled nipples. When I've had my fill and can't stand it any longer, I continue my descent as she rolls her hips into my touch, moaning beneath me. Leaning over her like this has my cock throbbing, begging to take more from her.

Stop! I mentally scream at myself. *Stop before you lose control.* I can't stop though, my hands aren't listening. One is running down her thigh while her pretty lips suck and tease the other in her sleep. Mustering all the control I can, I yank both hands away and take several steps back. Fuck trying not to wake her. I suck air in and out, panting loudly as I try to keep from coming in my pants. When it finally passes, I chastise myself for almost losing control and force myself to walk away. I have to leave. My time is more than up. I grab the menus off the small entry table and place them into the empty wooden mail holder on the kitchen counter near the coffeemaker. She's going to think she's more tired than she realized, not noticing and remembering things. When I've finished arranging them, I pull the card with a note out and use a magnet on the fridge to hang it up front and center. My poor little deer in headlights is going to think she's losing her mind. I can't wait to swoop in as the good guy caretaker tomorrow. I take one last look over everything, avoiding a glance in Hazel's direction, untrusting of myself and my intentions. Satisfied with a job well done, I slip on my boots and sneak back out the front door. There are four inches of fresh snow built up on the ground. I shovel my way back to the truck, once again concealing my footprints to be safe. When I climb inside, I turn the key over and let the engine warm up. While I do, I check the cameras to make sure she's still asleep.

My truck is facing the opposite direction of home, but I'm not touching that part of the road. I drive down to the next house, then use their long driveway to turn around. It's getting late and the plow still hasn't been by. I'm not disappointed if it keeps up. We're going to be trapped on the mountain in need of extra food. I set the plow down, clearing myself a path back up the mountain to my empty mansion to wait for her phone call. A dinner delivery is in my near future and I can't fucking wait.

Chapter 8

When I wake up, the cabin is steeped in shadows and darkness lurks around the edges of the room. Either I slept all day or the storm has worsened. I check the fireplace, which is still burning as though it's only been a few hours. I'll have to look outside. There's a giant window that runs two stories with the heavy curtains decadently descending from the ceiling to the floor. When I pull back a fold to peek out the streak-free perfect window, I'm disappointed to not only find two feet of snow, but the sun is setting on the west side of the house. Rich colors splash in through the opening I created, I rub my eyes, dropping the curtain back in place to stretch. The breakup zapped more of my energy than I realized. Or maybe I finally feel safe and relaxed enough to sleep. My stomach rumbles loudly and I check the time on my phone. It says I have a missed call from my dad and a voicemail. I also have five missed calls from Tyler and over fifty text messages. I decide the voicemail is the lesser of the two evils here, opting to handle it first. My stomach protests the choice loudly just as I realize it's five o'clock and I skipped a meal. I wonder how bad the snow is in the driveway. I force myself to walk to the front of the house, and when I open the door, I am pleasantly surprised to see the house lit up with Christmas lights, as if they are on some sort of timer. The twinkling red and green lights glow against the white fluffy snow continuing to fall from the sky, relentlessly covering the mountain. The driveway and front steps look like they were cleared at some point today because there's only about five inches piled up on them. I'm shocked I slept through someone clearing the driveway and front porch. It's actually a little terrifying. A shiver floods my body and I rub my arms.

It's definitely been coming down heavy the entire time I've been sleeping. I'm so tired I really don't feel like cooking, even though I asked them to stock the kitchen. Something not cooked by me sounds amazing. Tyler and I used to split the cooking, and doing it solo has been hard to get used to. I should probably be responsible and not make anyone venture out in this weather, but if one of the food places in town happened to be open—*it would mean it was safe, right?* Maybe I can find something online. I wander back to the kitchen, catching sight of all the snow on the deck through the French doors. I don't even think I can open them. The view is beautiful though. The sun is setting below the tree line of the forest. Snowflakes fall from the sky heavy and fast. Around me, in every direction, the white untouched snow flows endlessly. There's nowhere that remains untouched. It reminds me how alone I am up here. The snow is doing a great job of isolating me from the rest of the world, which is exactly what I wanted to do. My stomach rumbles again and I tear myself away from the view, turning and eyeballing the muffins before remembering how heavy of a meal they were. I'm sure there's more than enough food here that it would be easy to whip up something delicious for myself. The cupboard search begins once more, as I take stock of everything. I'm two cupboards deep when I notice the takeout menus in the wooden box next to the coffeemaker. Even my uncle doesn't want me to cook tonight. I smile, thinking of him. *What's the harm in looking?* It's strange I didn't notice these earlier when I was making coffee. It doesn't surprise me, though, given how hard I crashed. I pull out the menus and start sifting through them. When I find the pizza one, I punch in the numbers and wait for the phone to ring. Greasy, cheesy pizza sounds delicious and they usually deliver. The phone rings and I cross my fingers. Hopefully, they will deliver to this address. After the third ring, someone finally picks up.

"Y'ello, Mountain Pies, this is Tom. Delivery or pickup tonight?"

"Delivery," I stammer.

"Alright, it's going to be about ninety minutes for delivery right now," he responds.

"Ok," I answer. "Can I get a medium cheese pizza, garlic knots, and a Caesar salad, please?" I reply.

"Sounds good. Let me get your phone number in case we can't make it to your address, miss," he says.

I provide him the details and confirm I have enough cash for when he arrives. My stomach rumbles. An hour and a half is such a long time to wait. Knowing my luck, the snow will make it even longer and I'm starving. Maybe there's some fresh fruit in the fridge. I could use the natural sugar boost. As I reach to open it, I notice the card from earlier is hanging from a magnet. *Strange, I didn't leave you here.* I pull the card down and turn it over in my hands to inspect it. I glance around the room. Everything looks normal. The doors are all locked, and no one else is here. Clearly, I had to be the one to hang it up. I just don't remember doing it. My subconscious nags at me. I return it to the fridge, then pull the door open. Inside the fridge is a bin full of fresh apples, oranges, and pears. I grab an orange and start to peel it while walking back to the living room to check on the fire. I've burned through a fair amount of wood. Not enough to be concerned and I'm still confused about how that fire from earlier lasted all day. I must have slept for at least eight hours. Better to be thankful than to question things and freak myself out. Even if the fire hadn't lasted, I have regular heat. It's got to be at least 70 degrees in here now. I glance at the dwindling fire, trying to decide if I want to throw another log on. Ultimately, there's no reason not to. I slept all day, which means tonight will likely be a late night. I worry my lip for a few minutes, anxiously trying to decide if I want to commit to waiting for it to burn out. Well, I guess I could always just drizzle water and put it out, if it comes down to it. I grab three small pieces from the pile of wood and strategically build a much smaller fire, using the embers to slowly heat the new pieces. Eventually, they will get hot enough to ignite from one of the logs that's burning out. I poke at the embers one more time before deciding to wander around and pick out a bedroom for the night. Maybe I can unpack while I wait.

I traipse down the hallway, slurping my orange into my mouth. As the juice explodes in my mouth with a satisfying splash. There are two distinct sides to the house with the kitchen and giant living room, as well as the laundry and bathroom in the center. Upstairs used to have a loft and more rooms. I sneak down the hallway on my right in search of adventure, or maybe just a bed to sleep in tonight. The sectional wasn't bad, but a bed sounds much better for night number two. I stumble upon a small guest bedroom first. It's at the front of the house with an average bathroom attached. The space is crisp and cozy. It's a nice guest bedroom, but I really want the master bedroom experience. I continue down the hall to a spacious bonus room. Against one wall is a fully stocked bar, and on an opposite wall are massive bookcases, filled with books and knick-knacks. I smile to myself, getting lost in a memory from summers with my uncle. He used to love collecting treasures to add to his study. I wonder how many I can find from my childhood, though this might be an adventure for tomorrow. There's even a built-in cozy reading corner with one of those large bean bags. A small lounging sofa, an oversized desk, and a piano are also neatly placed throughout. The room opens up to a glass enclosed sunroom. I am so tempted to step inside when I see there's another fireplace and so many seating options with blankets and big, fluffy pillows. This room is definitely going on my list tomorrow. I've decided that after I build my snowman, I can warm up in here with read a good book. Skimming the shelves is going to be so fun. It looks like there's another set of doors leading out onto the back patio. I triple-check they are locked, all kinds of paranoid still. I chose to be alone, so I better get over whatever my brain has me freaking out over. With a sigh, I walk out of the room, deciding to make it a big part of my day tomorrow. I'm looking forward to something, and I can't help but feel a twinge of excitement and happiness in my broken heart.

There's a small, joyful bounce in my steps as I take my time retracing my way to the study. My exploring leads me to the other side of the cabin as I search for the main bedroom, beginning to plan out every detail in my mind. This hallway is much shorter, and I don't have time to think about things. At the end of the hallway is a set of double doors. *This must be it.* I bite my lip and push open both doors. When I step inside, my breath hitches. The main bedroom is fucking beautiful. There's a sitting area with a third fireplace. This one is outlined in the same floor-to-ceiling style and the brick is the same cracked pepper color as the living room. Once again, a stark contrast against the walnut-stained mantel and creamy white-gray walls. Heavy curtains matching the ones in the living room hide the giant windows in here, too. I spin around slowly, stopping only because my mouth drops open and my eyes bulge at the sight of the massive king-size bed. There's a giant light gray tufted headboard. The bed is slightly raised off the ground, not too high and not too low. I run my hands over the fluffy black feather-stuffed duvet and I have to fight the urge to fall into it. If my body touches the bed, I'm afraid I'll never get out. Across the bottom is another chunky-knit charcoal gray blanket, encouraging me to get lost in the cover. I squeal, not caring no one else can hear my eccentric celebration. I can't wait to go to sleep tonight.

"What the fuck?" I hiss, snapping out of whatever you would call daydreaming about sleeping in a bed. My eyes scan the neat stack of my luggage and suitcases next to the closet door.

What the fuck is going on? I'm completely and utterly confused. I don't remember unpacking, but then again, I also didn't plan to sleep for an entire day. Maybe I did unpack and I just don't remember from exhaustion. This feels insane, like I'm going crazy. I don't know what's going on, but I'm starting to question if I am mentally stable enough to be alone like this... It definitely feels like I am losing my mind. Maybe I should just journal this all really quickly so if it keeps happening I can call Mom. *So you can call Mom and then what?* I taunt myself. *Ask her to come up here? The roads are closed.* Fuck. The feelings of doubt are creeping in. I try to shake off the nervous feeling, hoping to avoid a panic attack, but I can already feel my heart thudding in my chest, beating rapidly as I take slow, steady breaths. This is just supposed to be a nice, much needed vacation. What does mom always say about water helping to relax? Maybe a shower will help me calm down, and I could probably use one. Even if it is just some random delivery person—I pause to smell my armpits. I didn't put deodorant on to sleep today, so I can one hundred percent benefit from freshening up. I check the time on my phone. There's still at least another thirty minutes before the pizza arrives.

Chapter 9

The bathroom is massive. There's a giant floor-to-ceiling shower with multiple shower heads. It even has the kind that shoots out of the wall. I turn on all the faucets I can find and wait for the water to get warm. The expensive-looking tile spans over the entire bathroom, which is the size of my bedroom at home. My gaze dashes over all the surfaces. There's a towel warmer next to the shower, and neatly in a small basket beside it is a pile of white fluffy towels. I pop one inside the warmer and turn it on, then begin to look around for soap. There's a control panel on the wall and the floors in this room are heated. I've never been spoiled like this before. It's glorious. Like my uncle spared no expense when he renovated. The dark walnut-stained exposed beams run throughout the house, creating an ambience like no other. Even in the bathroom, it adds a bit of character. Forgetting all about the warming shower, I drool over the oversized soaking tub. It's nestled in the corner with another large window spanning the length of the area with a recessed tiled ledge to place a candle. Against the other wall is a mounted television. Holy smokes! I can't believe there's a bathtub TV. I've finally found what I'm looking for—soap, and lots of it on the countertop. The tray is full to the brim with expensive looking soaps. *Are they handmade?* There are several shampoo and conditioner options, a loofa, and there's even some lotion. I grab a bar of soap, the loofa, and one each of the shampoo and conditioner, depositing them on the small shelf next to the shower. I'm in awe, shaking my head in disbelief as I continue to process the magnificence of the spa-inspired bathroom. Slowly, I undress before stepping into the shower and melting into the water, completely unprepared for the most relaxing shower imaginable.

The water washes down my body, rolling across my skin like warm fingers massaging me. It feels so good I never want it to end. Reaching for the shampoo, I lather it into my hair, enjoying the delicious smell of honey and vanilla. I take my time, letting the heat soak into my bones, and calming my nerves. Next I try the fancy soap. I work up a lather in the loofa, dragging the suds over my skin. I've never felt soap so soft, and the scent is delicious. This just might be the best shower I've ever taken. When I can't stand the water anymore and my fingers prune, I shut everything off and step out. The tile feels warm beneath the plushy foam bath mat, and I'm looking forward to the heated towel as I retrieve it from the warmer and wrap it around myself. A moan escapes my lips as I snuggle into the plush embrace. Once the towel cools off, I dry. While I do, I stare out the window in front of the tub, watching the snow fall from the sky.

I let out a surprised yelp and jump out of the view from the window. In the light from the Christmas lights glowing on the roof, I can just barely make out the large, burly man sitting on an ATV wearing a ski mask. He's on my property, and close enough that he is looking right at me. Or at least I assume he was staring at me. I wrap the towel around my naked body, then lean over to look out the window again. Sure enough, the man is staring back at me. He keeps me locked in his gaze as if he's holding me hostage, daring me to move out of his sight again. I'm not sure what has come over me as I stare him down while stepping back fully into view. I swear I see him wink at me and some part of me that's inanely reckless snaps. *Fuck it.* I slide the towel sensually across the round curves of my breasts and down until I'm standing there bare chested, flashing him. He licks his lips, or at least that's what I imagine he's doing—because I am imagining this, right? Either way, it only encourages me more. I slide the towel down my waist seductively, but just as I am about to drop it to the ground, my phone chimes. A message from the pizza place pops up, saying my driver should arrive soon. I jump, snatching the towel back around myself and hurry into the bedroom, passing a small storage shelf with a fluffy robe folded neatly on top of it. Out of sight in the bedroom, I wrap the robe around myself, close my eyes, and take a deep breath. I'm most definitely having a panic attack and there's no way in hell a relaxing shower will calm me down from this one. What the fuck is going on? There was a man there, wasn't there? Why the fuck did I do that? It's practically inviting trouble to hang out. I'm too terrified to make sure he's actually gone, but I convince myself to be brave. I flip off the lights and slink against the wall, peering out the window, searching for any shape that could be mistaken for a man on an ATV, but there's no one outside. The doorbell rings and I damn-near jump right out of my skin. Frustrated with my imagination, I return to the entryway where I left my purse and pull out the amount I need to pay the driver. I'm extremely grateful they drove out here, and I don't mind tipping a little extra. I pull the sash tighter, securing the robe, before my fingers brush over the metal lock, turning it slowly and pulling open the door.

Thank my lucky stars it's an ordinary-looking pizza man with one of those creepy mustaches decorating his top lip. I yank the door open wider to accept the pizza, shoving the cash at him as I do. He hands over the pizza, garlic knots, and a bag with what I assume is my salad.

"Thank you," I stammer, uncomfortably. I intentionally ordered a lot so they wouldn't suspect I was alone.

"Pizza's here." I pretend to shout as if there are others waiting for the hot meal.

I start to close the door, "Have a good night," the man says with a wink, as he begins descending the front path.

Oh shit! Someone shoveled the entire front sidewalk and driveway again. I slam the door and lock it behind him, then hurry to the kitchen to set the pizza down. I walk briskly back to the main bathroom to check one more time to see if the man is still there—only I'm not sure what I will do if he is. *Why am I not calling the cops?* The voice in my head is loud and clear as it sounds several alarms. Yet I continue my quest to see if the man waited for me to return.

In the bathroom, I look out the window. It's only been a few minutes, but it's so much darker than it was a few minutes ago. I squint into the shadows, looking for him, but there's nothing there. I probably scared him off when I ran. *Oh well,* I think, stepping into the large tub to pull the blinds down. A thought strikes me and I find myself suddenly mortified. What if that was the caretaker, and oh gosh—I need to call tomorrow about the firewood! If he was the one who shoveled... I groan. This might be embarrassing. I'm not sure whether to feel better about the possibility that it wasn't a creepy stranger, and might actually be the caretaker doing his job. On a positive note, it would also explain what I thought I saw last night and why someone was hanging around the cabin. I feel myself relaxing. I may as well also thank them for the muffins, then find out if there is more wood somewhere on the property. Venturing out in the snow like a kid might be fun. I smile to myself, deciding it's a date. Tomorrow I am going to build a snowman and go in search of wood. It will be an epic day and I will not sleep away another day of my vacation. I'm living in the here and now, I remind myself. I practically have the entire day planned for tomorrow. It feels good to have something to look forward to.

As a calm settles over me, I return to the bedroom in search of my pajamas. I open a few looking for comfortable pajama pants and a T-shirt. When I locate them, I dress quickly, then make my way to the kitchen, where I can smell the greasy cheese and tomato sauce waiting for me. I grab a diet Dr. Pepper from the fridge and sit down at the island, flipping the box open. I don't even bother with a plate, digging right in, enjoying the way the hot cheese and grease drip down my chin. Tyler would never be okay with me eating something so unhealthy. I snicker, if he could only see me now eating more than one slice *and* drinking soda. Thinking about him reminds me to do something about all his text messages. I'm not all that interested in reading them, but I open my phone, skimming through each one. I can't believe what I am reading. He claims he's going to drive up here if he doesn't hear from me soon. I don't want him to do that. The last thing I need is him ruining my relaxing retreat. I fire off a quick reply, telling him not to come and reminding him I don't want to talk to him.

"We are over, Tyler. For good this time. Stop texting me and let me go."

I block his phone number, hoping that solves my Tyler problem once and for all. In retrospect, I should have done it a long time ago. I'm ready to heal. I thought being alone would terrify me, but there's something thrilling about the unknown. I wonder if the caretaker is hot? Maybe he can be my cheesy Christmas happily ever after. I laugh at myself before shoving a garlic knot in my mouth and devouring it.

Kane

Chapter 10

Last night was incredible. She fucking flashed me. Hazel stood naked right in front of me and I've never felt more alive. It took every ounce of restraint not to shove my way through the front door and rip that robe off her body. She probably thought the pizza delivery guy was an asshole, but if only she knew how hard it was to maintain my composure after our little encounter. Stupid pre-scheduled text had to go and mess up everything. I wonder how far she would have gone if my stupid fake text hadn't interrupted us. I was killing some time, shoveling and plowing again while the delivery minutes ticked down. Of course, I didn't plan on watching her shower. It was a bit of a happy coincidence and once I started watching her, I couldn't pull my eyes away. My mind was racing, imagining the way she was rubbing the cum-laced soap all over her body and through her hair. Hazel quite literally bathed in my cum and even now, just thinking about it has me so turned on. Last night left me more sexually frustrated than I've ever been, but it also taught me something interesting about my girl. There's no arguing about it either. The girl of my dreams is into some crazy shit, which is good to know because so am I. In fact, I'm into some really freaky stuff and I stayed up all night plotting out an insane sexcapade to act out together. Unable to help myself, I reach down and adjust my erection. *I want her so bad.*

No.

I need her so bad.

Waiting is going to be torture today. My eyes sweep over the Christmas gift bag taunting. As I lean against the cool marble countertops in my kitchen, I advert my gaze and stir my home-brewed peppermint mocha. 'Tis the season for candy canes and cocoa. Why shouldn't that include my coffee? I take a gulp, then release a satisfying sigh. Today is the day I get to feel Hazel's slick little pussy, wet for me and clenching around my cock while I pound her into falling in love with me. The last two days have dragged on for what feels like forever but the weather is perfect today, and I have all the pieces to my plan set up. Including a special little furry surprise, all for my naughty little Christmas elf.

Before my imagination can start wandering all over again, I turn back around and return to frosting the cookies I baked for her. My knife slides a thick layer of frosting across the last few before I place each of them on the plate next to the others. Once the plate is full and overflowing, I sprinkle them all with a little crushed up molly I mixed into red and green sugar sprinkles. Pulling plastic wrap over the top, I slide them next to the gift bag. This morning I got up bright and early to bake these extra special cookies for Hazel. My secret ingredient is fresh morning cum and just enough Molly to encourage her to let loose. I check the clock for the millionth time as I work on cleaning up, and before I can remind myself that patience is a virtue, my phone rings.

It's her. I swallow hard, answering confidently. "Mountainside Management, this is Kane. How can I help you?" My tone is cheery and fake.

"Hi, uh, um," she stammers awkwardly, and fuck if it doesn't get me even harder hearing the sound of her voice and knowing what I plan to do to her today. "I am staying at my uncle's place and I am just wondering where can I get some more firewood from? Is there a place in town or a pile somewhere? I didn't want to go wandering out in the snow without asking first."

"It's your lucky day. I was just on my way out the door to plow the snow. How about I swing by and bring some up from beneath the deck for you? There's a huge pile under a tarp on the downstairs patio." I reply, trying my best to stay calm.

"Oh, it's no bother. I can run down and get it. Please don't trouble yourself. The muffins and coffee were so thoughtful. I can't thank you enough for stocking the cabin for my stay," she replies.

"It's no problem at all. I am happy to get it for you. Your uncle was a good friend of mine. I hope you'll decide to keep the cabin. It would be a shame to see it go to a stranger." I bite my tongue, instantly realizing the stranger comment was a slip. I hope she doesn't catch on.

"If you insist. Let me at least offer you some coffee or cocoa. Honestly, it's the least I can do. I assume it's you who has been shoveling and keeping all the snow cleared."

"Guilty," I reply, clearing my throat.

"Then I definitely would like to make you a cup of something to show how appreciative I am that you've been taking care of all the snow since I arrived. Consider it a tip for setting up the cabin," she practically begs.

"What kind of grinch would I be if I turned down a cup of cocoa this close to Christmas? You drive a hard bargain, but if you make the cocoa, I'll bring some cookies down with me for you to enjoy later. I was up early baking this morning and made a big batch." I'm laying on my charm real thick.

"You bake?!" She says, surprised. "Wow, I've never met a man who bakes. I guess that explains the muffins."

Her voice is airy and light, almost flirty. *Of course, it is. She's sad, lonely, and dreaming of a Christmas love story.* I roll my eyes at myself and then drop my voice an octave. "That's not all I'm good at. You might say I'm a Jack-of-all-trades, the perfect kind of guy to keep around."

The line is silent. Shit, I scared her off. I clear my voice and try to recover. "For the management company, I mean, because it makes me fantastic at my job as caretaker, ya know?"

"Oh yes, that makes lots of sense," she replies, laughing nervously.

"I better get the truck warmed up. I'll see you in, let's say, fifteen minutes? Is that enough time for you to get some cocoa made?"

"It's plenty of time," she replies, her tone more relaxed again.

"Great. I can't wait to meet Dex's niece. See you soon." I hang up, not wanting to risk slipping up again.

It's time to go meet Hazel and though we've met several times now, it's the first time she gets to meet me as myself. I'm dying to be close to her—to interact with her—and with any luck, make her fall in love with me. This should be easy enough. I've taken all the correct steps to get her up here, isolated and all alone with me. She's heartbroken, vulnerable, and easy to manipulate, or at least I hope she is. My cock strains at the thought of her being vulnerable. *I know, buddy, I can't wait either.*

It's a good thing the truck has a remote start, because I'm a mess from baking despite wearing this festive holiday apron. I press the start button and wait to hear the truck's engine roar before peeling the apron off and tossing it in the laundry bin as I walk upstairs to change my clothes.

I pull on a fitted red, waffle-knit sweater with a white snowflake printed on the front, a matching plaid Christmas scarf, a pair of thermal pants, and some dark designer jeans. Back downstairs, I slip on my boots and a thermal-lined beanie. It's freezing out there, and I'm not worried about styling my hair today, not when I'll be hunting later. Once I'm all bundled up again, I drive down to the cabin, nervous I might accidentally slip and overshare again, but determined not to. When I climb out of the truck, she's on the front porch decked out in winter gear and waiting, like she plans to help.

"Hi," she waves, "I'm Hazel. Thank you for the welcome basket."

"Nice to meet you, Hazel. I'm Kane," I reply, flashing her a toothy smile. "You're welcome. I'll take care of all the snow. You don't need to worry about helping me." I wave before turning my back to her and grabbing my shovel.

"Hey, can I ask you a weird question?"

"Sure," I reply.

"This might sound crazy, but would you, by chance, have been out on your ATV on my property last night?" Her voice is shaky and nervous.

I have to force my face muscles not to react. I want to smile and bask in the glory of what she's actually asking me. *Which is, "Did I strip for you last night and then did you go home and jerk off to the saved video footage from the camera in the bathroom?"* And if Hazel asked me that, I would have a very hard time denying it.

"No, why? Did you hear something?" I ask, trying to act concerned.

"I actually thought I saw something—or someone." She replies.

"Hmm. It's probably nothing, but if you want me to go out and ride the property line looking for tracks, I don't mind. With the roads nearly impassible, I doubt the sheriff could even make it out here."

She shudders when I mention that sheriff. Fuck if it doesn't satisfy me in some weird way.

"I'll pass on calling the sheriff. If you don't mind checking the property line, I really would appreciate it."

"You got it, Ms. Hazel. Not a problem at all. I'll be back in no time for that cup of cocoa."

"I'll be here." She says, waving before stepping back inside.

I wave back. *Ahhh, Kane, you sly dog. Offering to look for tracks makes the perfect excuse for why your ATV tracks are on her property. No one will argue with the video her doorbell camera just recorded either. My alibi is airtight, as usual. I'm too good at this.*

Later, I'll do a clean pass of me walking to the truck and starting it, so on the camera footage it shows I left. Then I'll walk the cookies back in, and last but not least, plant my Christmas gift for Hazel on the porch. When I get home,

I'll erase all the footage and wait for her to call me. It's perfect, absolutely nothing can go wrong.

Chapter 11

Since Kane is obviously some kind of amazing chef who also fucking bakes, his offer to ride the property line and check on things was the opportunity I needed to buy myself more time to make something better than microwave cocoa. Inside the kitchen, I peer out the window overlooking the deck. Kane's red beanie sticks out against the stark white terrain. Snow coats every surface and it's so cold that even the water in the air is freezing, making it appear as if it's snowing when it's really not. Down to business, though. I have enough time, but I don't have extra time to get lost in my thoughts about snow and ice crystals. My phone dings on the counter, but rather than check my message, I tap open the internet and type in a quick search for homemade hot cocoa. I click on a few different recipes to compare methods. It's actually a lot easier than I realized. I just need milk, chocolate, and vanilla.

Time to hunt through the kitchen. I find the vanilla with the baking supplies easily. I also happen upon some fancy chocolates in the same cupboard. They look like they were handmade, likely by Kane. They are wrapped in clear cellophane bags, sealed, and each one has a Christmas-themed tag identifying the type of chocolate inside tied around it with a red or green ribbon. *Holy shit! This guy really goes all out, and he wasn't kidding about being good at his job.* I examine each of the bags, but one in particular catches my eye. White chocolate, peppermint bark. Perfect for Candy Cane Cocoa, it says. I chuckle softly. That's pretty cute.

Perfect for cocoa. This will surely score me some points with Kane. I snatch the peppermint bark and then grab milk from the fridge. On the stove, I warm a saucepan on low and place several large pieces of peppermint bark in it to melt. Then I go in search of toppings and retrieve the whipped cream from the fridge. From the baking cupboard I grab mini marshmallows, and from the card on the counter I pull off the peppermint candy cane taped to the front. Using a glass from the cupboard, I smash the candy cane into tiny decorative pieces for the top. All the while I check the chocolate, stirring it as needed before looking out the window, watching for Kane to return. Once the chocolate melts, I slowly pour in the milk like the directions say, and add the vanilla extract. Then I stir slowly until it's smooth and creamy. There's still no sign of Kane, so I turn the burner down to the fancy low-melt temperature on the knob and throw another log on the fire. I've kept it burning since I arrived and I'm not the least bit ashamed to admit it. Before I sit down to curl up on the sectional, I peek out the window, searching for a little red dot.

Instead of spotting his hat, I'm surprised to see his ATV parked in the yard near the stairs of the deck. *That was fast.* He must be grabbing the firewood I asked him about. Instead of wrapping up in a blanket, I scurry to the kitchen to check on the cocoa and stir it. All the toppings are lined up on the island, waiting for assembly. There are a variety of cup options, too, since I'm not sure if he intends to stay for cocoa, or if he's planning to use a to-go cup. I don't want to make this into something it's not—but a holiday romance is exactly what I'm looking for and I would literally do anything to live out that fantasy.

A knock on the glass patio door makes me jump. I turn around quickly, then breathe a sigh of relief when I realize it's just Kane holding several bundles of firewood and another pile by his feet. My cheeks flush with embarrassment over my reaction to his knocking. I walk over and unlock the door. Up close, he's even more overwhelming.

The man is huge. His muscular arms and shoulders are broad, and his stance fills the entire doorway. I stare at him for a moment taking everything about him in from the way his chestnut-colored hair peeks out from beneath his beanie, to his perfectly shaped lips—full in all the right places—the kind that are irresistible and feel like heaven when they kiss you. He's tall, too, easily over six and a half feet. This man is definitely large enough he could overpower me if he wanted to, but there's something about the twinkle in his eyes and the laid back tone of his voice that makes me feel at ease.

"Mind if I bring these in for you?" He asks, interrupting my silent assessment.

My cheeks flush. "Yes, I'm so sorry. I don't know what came over me. You're just so different from what I was expecting."

Kane chuckles. "Yeah, I get that reaction a lot. When people think of caretakers, and maintenance men, I'm not exactly sure what they conjure up."

"I'm so sorry. I didn't mean to offend you. It's just, well, I don't know what I was thinking."

"No need to be sorry. But I need to set this down."

"Of course." I step aside, allowing him to squeeze in through the door.

He sets the first bundle inside on the rubber mat next to the door, then goes back out for the other pile. This time, he slips off his shoes and walks to the fireplace. He moves around as if he owns the place. At first it feels a little weird, but then I remember he said he was friends with my uncle, and obviously he takes care of the property, so it makes sense that he would know where everything is. I watch him mindlessly stirring the cocoa. He's every-thing a woman could dream of in a holiday romance—tall, handsome, and muscular. I bet he has a six-pack under all those layers. Kane's charming and bearded, plus he knows his way around a kitchen. Where has he been all my life? *Don't do this, Hazel. Don't get attached to a fantasy idea of a romance. Besides, someone as attractive as him is probably married.*

While I try to get a look at his hands for a wedding ring, Kane goes about his business, putting the wood away and rebuilding the fire. At first I'm offended, because how dare he insult my fire-building skills, but then I figure he's just a nice guy, probably trying to be helpful. Maybe I need to relax. The poor guy might be lonely for all I know.

"Hey, so are there any big plans today?" I ask him, in an attempt at casual conversation.

"Nothing too out of the ordinary. How about you?" He asks.

I shrug my shoulders. "Nothing major, I'll probably watch a Christmas movie, explore my uncle's office a little. Maybe find a good book to curl up with and try out the glass room with the other fireplace."

"Well, doesn't that sound like the perfect day? Don't let me forget to leave you some of those cookies I baked. I make them on the healthier side with extra proteins baked in." He flexes his muscles. "Ya know, gotta stay fit in this line of work." He winks playfully.

"Would you like to stay for a movie with the cocoa?" *Crap, the words slipped out of my mouth and I can't take them back. What am I doing?*

He smiles at me. "That's really nice of you—"

I interrupt him before he can finish. "Oh gosh, I'm so sorry. I didn't mean anything by it. I'm sure you're married, or have a girlfriend, and I don't mean it like that. I just...I over share sometimes, and my mom has always said I'm too nice to people, and oh god now I'm rambling."

I clap my hands over my mouth, mortified. *OMG, Hazel, you're a fucking idiot. It was a wonder you landed a guy like Tyler—or maybe it wasn't since he turned out to be fake perfect. Stop it.* I think I'm losing my fucking mind. This man is making me crazy and awkward. Why am I like this, and how is it fair to blame him? I really need to get a grip.

Kane laughs and wow, his laugh is incredible. "It's okay, I'm also a bit on the neurospicy side. But nope, no girlfriend or wife to be jealous. I was going to say I would love to, but only if I get to pick."

I laugh nervously. "Great, make yourself comfortable and pick a movie. I'm pretty sure my uncle has every channel and subscriptions to every streaming service imaginable. I'll grab the cocoa. Are you okay with marshmallows, whipped cream, and candy canes?"

"Hazel, I'm okay with anything, as long as it tastes good."

I'm not sure why the way he says my name sends a tingle through my core, but it does, and I can't help but imagine this turning into an adorable meet-cute story.

Chapter 12

Spending the morning with Kane was nice and refreshing. It helps that he is a total hottie. There's just something about his deep voice that puts me at ease. I could listen to him talk all day—honestly, the man should narrate a goddamn audiobook. Once I calmed down and stopped acting like a total embarrassment in front of him, we had the best time talking about our favorite parts in the movie and naming our other favorite holiday movies. Turns out, we have a lot in common in the holiday movie department. He's nice, too. Not only did he check the property line and report it clear of any tracks, but he also offered to fix me a sandwich since—according to him—I'm on vacation and I deserve a little break. I told him about the pizza, offering him leftovers but he insisted on making me something fresh. He knows most of the restaurants won't be delivering before everyone on the mountain has had some time to dig out. Kane even said if the roads are still bad in the morning, he wouldn't mind coming down to make breakfast, or picking me up to eat at his place. He has a home theater, and he suggested a movie marathon. Maybe he has mistletoe and he'll kiss me under it too, and then we will fall madly in love. *What about Tyler?* My heart cries.

I'm done with Tyler. This is my chance at a holiday romance, the good karma I deserve after he cheated on me. So what if none of this is practical? Sure, maybe it sounds a tad delusional but it's exactly what I need to get over Tyler— or I fear my heart will never heal. We'd been together for four years, and it feels like the ultimate betrayal. How could he do this to me after asking me to pick up my entire life and move away with him? I thought we were in love. A teardrop escapes, rolling slowly down my cheek. Then another, and another. Pretty soon I'm crying my eyes out next to the still warm and crackling fire. Why did it have to be like this?

Sighing, I dry my tears, take a deep breath and wander into the kitchen for one of those delicious-looking cookies. I select a Christmas tree-shaped one and take a bite. The cookie melts in my mouth. It's the perfect combination of soft with a bit of crisp on the outside. It has the faintest flavor of peppermint to it, and mixed with the vanilla undertones in the sugar cookie, it gives my tastebuds an orgasm of their own. Kane must have been a chef in his past life, because these cookies are far too scrumptious for him to be an amateur baker. I savor each bite and then select another. This time opting for a fancy reindeer, complete with a Red Hot for its nose. If I don't get away from these cookies soon, I'm going to end up wearing them all. I stand from where I was perched on a chair at the kitchen island. Deciding that getting lost in the pages of a book is exactly the distraction my brain needs. The sun is falling in the afternoon sky, which means it should be directly pouring into the glass room I so desperately wanted to explore. I stuff my phone into my pocket and nibble my cookie as I meander my way to Uncle Dexter's office. My plans for curling up with a book consume my thoughts. As outside, the sun fights its way through the swirling snow that is falling from the sky again. *Man, did I underestimate the storm*. But I wouldn't change this for anything. Everything about this place is quiet and serene. And now that I've met Kane, it's giving me something to at least fantasize about—no matter how unhealthy my therapist might say this is.

When I step into the office's attached sunroom, I look around in awe at his bookshelves. It's a two-story room, which I didn't notice last time. The upper level is filled with rows of bookshelves. Downstairs there are double French doors that lead to the sunroom. The beautiful piano I noticed my first time in here rests regally in a sitting area. It looks like it has never been played. My fingers flex at the thought, remembering all those piano lessons my mom and dad paid for. Immediately, I'm drawn to it, pausing only to run my fingers over small familiar trinkets from my time spent here on rainy days as a child. I remember Uncle Dexter and I used to play our own version of hide-and-seek where I used to wander around until something caught my eyes, then I would bring it to him and he would tell me all about how the object came to live in his office. I used to love listening to his stories about the places he traveled and the people he met. My fingers brush over a rock on the edge of his desk and read the messy scrawled letters that spell out *I love you*. My heart twinges with the pain of the memory. I made that for him the last summer I spent up here because I wanted him to have a special paperweight. That year was especially windy and one day when I came bursting in from the patio—where the sunroom is now—his papers blew everywhere and made such a mess. I felt terrible for days and this rock that I rolled all the way up from the lake was my attempt to say I was sorry and make things right. Uncle Dexter was never mad at me to begin with, though, and thinking about it now, that's probably why I felt so bad. He was completely unfazed by the mess, and instead made a game of picking up all the papers with me while pretending to be a pirate hunting a treasure. My heart is missing him. I miss that I never got to experience those moments again after the falling out—and I hate that I never made time for him in my adult life until the end.

Before I start to cry again, I let my fingers fall from the smooth surface of the rock and walk over to the piano. The temptation to tap out a tune on the keys is too overpowering to resist. I slide into position on the bench, wiggle my butt, and sit up straight. It's been a long time since I've played the piano, but I think I can still play Heart and Soul. I'm trying for the umteenth time to get the correct note when the doorbell rings.

That's odd, I think for all of five seconds before playing out an entire scene in my head where I open the door to find the very handsome, very charming Kane standing on the doorstep. *Hello, sexy caretaker. Are you here to take care of my needs?* I think to myself, before the bell rings a second time. I rush to the front door and swing it open, thinking nothing of who or what might be on the other side, only hoping that it is Kane I find on the other side. To my disappointment, there's no one at the door. There is, however, a gift bag on the porch with a card on top addressed to me. *How strange.* It's one of those extra fancy bags and as I step forward from the safety of the doorway to retrieve it, I suddenly become hyper-aware that the sender could still be watching me. With an abundance of caution, I pick the bag up gingerly and step back inside, twisting the deadbolt into the locked position behind me. As I dive into the contents, not bothering to open the card first, my face falls. Could this be from Tyler? He's supposed to be in Florida, but who else would send something like this? There's also the chance that it's the wrong house and maybe not even intended for me. *God, I really hope blocking Tyler didn't fuel the fire, and he didn't come up here.* I don't want to see him. I'm not sure I'm strong enough to walk away a second time.

My mind is racing in a million directions and I'm feeling all kinds of strange conflicting feelings for Tyler, or maybe I'm thinking about Kane. I don't know. Everything feels like it's whooshing around me—as if the world is passing me by—and all I want is a happily ever after. I pull the card out, needing to know who sent this. My finger slides gracefully across the paper to reveal a Christmas card. I flip it open to read the greeting. Below the standard holiday wishes in every Christmas card ever printed, my eyes stumble across the messy handwriting. I read the words over a few times and instantly assume it has to be from Tyler, but after intensely studying it for I don't know how long, I realize the handwriting looks nothing like his. The note reads:

Put this on and don't think twice. You've been naughty instead of nice.

It must be from Kane—or maybe I just desperately want my incredibly handsome caretaker to also be my secret admirer. My hands tug the paper out at rapid speed, pulling out the sexy lingerie set, which ends up falling out of its wrapping and landing at my feet. I bend down to retrieve it, genuinely curious as to what it's supposed resemble, so I casually undress in the middle of the entryway, no longer worried about who might have left it on my step.

Once I've squeezed into the skimpy little outfit, I race to the bathroom for a look in the mirror, and to clip the adorable little furry ears with jingle bells into my ponytail. For a reindeer outfit, it's pretty cute. The brown mesh bra top lends itself to being see-through, while the black leather jingle bell-lined band encircles my chest. The straps are also black with jingle bells. There's a sheer lace thong beneath the super-short pleated, faux leather skirt that doesn't completely ride up my ass and feels like it was designed for a woman with more curves like myself. Turning in the mirror, I notice my ass cheeks are hanging out like crazy. For once, I actually feel sexy in lingerie. I'm not the least bit ashamed of my reflection. It's like whoever sent it knows their way around a woman with curves. I grab my phone and snap a few sexy photos. I'm not above posting these to hurt Tyler... or maybe I should *accidentally* send them to hottie caretaker Kane. *Would he drive down here in his truck to ravish me?* I grin. Maybe it's actually from Kane, because the things Tyler bought for me never made me feel sexy or confident. My heart beats faster. Another clue that it's not Tyler. I actually squeal. I can feel the dampness in the thong panties as I let the excitement sink in and I'm still admiring myself in the mirror when I hear a loud thud coming from the backdoor, I let out a scream. Terrified someone is breaking in to have their way with me. Or maybe that's just what I want to happen. The adrenaline pumps through my body as I race through the house to the backdoor, hoping to find myself a good time.

I scream again. This time it's a blood-curdling, heart-wrenching scream. My body shakes. To my horror, there is a large deer lying on the back porch. It probably ran right into the glass, not realizing it was there. With the blowing snow, it's hard to see anything. My heart drops when I realize it's not getting back up. I stand there in complete panic, unsure of what to do or who to call.

I'm frozen in time, staring at the unmoving animal, watching for signs of life, anything. But the giant creature continues to lay still. My phone is in the bathroom where I left it when I ran out here. I slowly back my way into the hall, not wanting to tear my eyes away from the animal. When I reach the protection of the long hallway, I turn on my heels, bolting to the bathroom to grab my phone. I don't know who to call. Do I call the police? A shudder runs over me. No. That sheriff is way too creepy. I hope I never see him again for as long as I live. Do I call my parents? *What would they do, Hazel? It's not like they can drive up here, genius.* Except there is someone who said if I need anything, to simply give them a call.

I dash to the fridge where Kane's business card is held up by a clip magnet. My fingers tremble as I punch in the numbers on the phone. When it finally connects, the phone rings and rings. I hold my breath, waiting for the person on the other line to answer. Praying he picks up.

Kane

Chapter 13

Right on cue, Hazel calls me. It was pretty obvious watching her on the cameras that the Molly was kicking in, which meant it was finally time to put my plan in motion.

I let my phone ring a few times and then picked it up. "Mountainside Management, this is Kane. How—" She interrupts me before I can finish.

"Kane," she says, her voice shaking. "Something strange happened. There's a deer on the back deck, and it's not moving."

"A deer?" I repeat, pretending to be shocked. "Is there anything wrong with it? Any injuries? Did you call the police?"

"I... well, I'm not sure what to do. I didn't know if I should call the police, or if it's just my problem to get rid of now." She answers frantically.

"It's okay. I'll come right down and then we can figure it out." I soothe.

She chokes on her words, a sob building in her throat. The fear in her voice making my dick hard. All I can think about is how soon I'm going to be inside of her tight, wet pussy.

"I... please... Don't call the cops. The sheriff is terrifying." Her voice cracks, and my dick gets even harder.

"It's okay, I'm on my way. It won't take me long to get there. Do you think you can try looking out the window to see if it's injured?" I ask, innocently.

"I can try," she stammers.

"Listen, I didn't want to say anything to scare you, but I haven't been entirely honest about why I've been hanging around either." I confess.

She's silent.

"What?" she finally asks. "What do you mean?"

I can hear the disappointment in her voice. "Look," I continue. "I think you should eat something and sit down so I don't catch you off guard. I don't need you fainting on me. Why don't you go try one of those cookies I baked you and go sit by the fireplace?"

I know full well she's already had two of my cum cookies with extra special frosting. Part of me just wants to know she's eating my cum while I talk to her and the other part of me wants to make sure the drugs don't wear off until after I've had my fun with her.

"I've already had two," she confesses uncomfortably.

My dick flexes. Fuck, that really turns me on. I have to bite my knuckle to keep from groaning.

"So have another. Darling, you're gorgeous, and anyone who tells you otherwise isn't worth it."

I can see her on my screen, biting her lip nervously. Fucking bastard. Tyler deserves what he got, just for ruining her self-esteem. So what if Hazel has a curvy body? I like my thighs thick.

She does what I tell her and I watch on screen as she enters the kitchen, retrieves the cookie, then sits next to the fire. She takes a few nibbles. "Okay, I'm ready." Hazel squeaks out. "Tell me whatever it is."

"Promise you won't hang up on me." I demand.

"Okay." She answers.

"Okay, what?" I coax.

"I promise I won't hang up on you. Come on, it can't be that bad."

I hesitate before blurting out what I want to tell her. "There's a serial killer loose on the mountain."

She gasps, then screams. Even though I know she's reacting to my news and not in any danger, I have to play along.

"Hazel, are you okay? Why are you screaming? Talk to me. Tell me what's happening." I probe, feigning a concerned tone.

"Why didn't you think this would be important to tell someone? Why didn't you call me and tell me not to come? Would we be safer together?" She fires off her questions rapidly.

If only she knew being with me was more dangerous than being alone. I roll my eyes, annoyed by her questions. The answers are so obvious. I didn't tell her because you don't just shake someone's hand and say, "Hi, I'm a serial killer, I invited her to stay alone for a reason and calling to cancel would have ruined everything." *Duh.*

"There's no time for that. I need you to get a closer look at the deer. I didn't want it to come to this, but the serial killer has been leaving dead animals on his victim's porches. Like a calling card of sorts." I hold my breath, waiting for her response.

"What should I do? I'm all alone." She's trembling as I watch her on the screen.

"I know, Hazel. I promise. I'm on my way. Put on your boots, grab your jacket, and if there's any sign of trauma, any sort of injury, promise me one thing. Promise me you'll run. Get to the path behind the cabin and follow the shoreline of the lake. I'll meet you. He could be inside already. I promise I will get to you. I'm grabbing my ATV now." My directions are calm, despite everything I am telling her to do.

"Stay on the phone with me, please," she begs.

"I can't. I need two hands to drive if you want me to get to you. You're going to have to be brave and trust me. I promised your uncle I would keep you safe, and I never break my promises." My attempt to reassure her seems to work.

She nods her head in agreement. "Okay. I'll see you as soon as you get here."

"I'll see you soon, Hazel. I promise. I'll see you soon."

Chapter 14

What the fuck am I doing? I'm wearing nothing but the sexy lingerie as I shove my feet into snow boots and toss my jacket on, zipping it. The moment Kane said the serial killer could be inside the house, I knew that any possibility of changing back into my clothes went right out the window. I need to get the fuck out of here. Fast! That's not my only reason for skipping the clothing change, though, and I know it. I'm not sure what's come over me, but all I can think about is sleeping with Kane. It's crazy the way I could be in actual danger, and yet all I can think about is seducing the sexy caretaker-turned-knight-in-shining-armor on his way to rescue me from a killer. I hope he finds this ridiculous outfit irresistible. My eyes glaze over as I imagine what it might feel like for his full and sensual lips to kiss me, dragging across my skin, igniting my senses.

I shiver, snapping out of it and cross the room to the back door. It takes me another few minutes to talk myself into opening it because once again, I've trapped myself in a fantasy with Kane. My sweaty fingers grip the door handle as I stand frozen in fight-or-flight mode. Inside my chest, my heart is racing. It beats so loudly it's the only thing I can hear as my senses zero in on the hypnotic rhythm. Outside, the snow is falling so hard there's a fresh dusting on the deer. Finally, I work up the courage to unlock the door, and I step outside to get a better look at the animal. Slowly, while keeping a close eye on my surroundings, I inch my way closer, body shaking. It's not moving at all, and the closer I get, the more I notice the snow is tinted pink. I clasp my hands over my mouth and feel my stomach wretch. It's pink because of the blood mixed in the snow. It's hard, but I force myself to keep going. As I inch closer to the area where the animal rests, injured, the bloody spots get darker. Eventually, once I reach the far side of the deck, I realize the poor beautiful creature was impaled with a giant icicle. *Maybe it's not a serial killer and the poor thing genuinely ran into the door, causing an icicle to fall and then, boom, death.*

I've nearly convinced myself that is exactly what happened, and it's merely an accident, but then I spot words. Bright red, scrolling words. There's a trail of bloody footprints and someone has used the animal's blood to write a message in the snow.

Shit! It *is* the serial killer. *Stay calm.* I tell myself, but it's too late. I'm already panicking.

I look toward the cabin, then to the shoreline of the lake. *Trust me,* Kane said. I take a deep breath, walking toward the bloody writing despite every instinct in my body screaming at me not to. It reads:

Run, little Jane Doe. Don't look back.

I start to yelp, then clamp my mouth closed. Breathing heavily into my hands. I'm most definitely having a panic attack. Jane Doe? Didn't the sheriff call me that? I want to scream for Kane, to stand here and wait for him to appear to whisk me away—or better yet, I want to wake up and realize all of it, even the part about Tyler cheating, is all a damn dream. That's it. This must be a dream. There's no way stuff like this happens in real life. *Except I know far too well that stuff like this* definitely *happens in real life.*

My fingers are freezing cold. I didn't bring gloves and I'm not going back now. I blow on them as I stumble through the accumulated snow, working my way over to examine the writing. There's no avoiding it. I have to walk past the writing to get to the stairs and now that I'm standing right in front of it, my feet are frozen, unwilling to move. The crimson color stains the glistening white snow and I can feel my stomach threatening to regurgitate the cookies I just ate. In the distance, I can hear what sounds like a motor. It's probably Kane—at least I hope it's him—barreling to rescue me. When I stop to think about it, this is exactly what I asked for—albeit, a much darker holiday romance than I was hoping for. I sigh, squeezing my eyes shut, mentally pushing myself to walk past all the blood and down the stairs.

Once my feet hit the bottom of the steps, I turn and take off, running in the direction of the shoreline. The snow is freezing cold as it encircles my legs, creeping up far higher than my boots cover. Against my skin, the cold stings. The snow is deep and though I'm trying to move through it quickly. I know I must look ridiculous in my attempt to run but the snow is so heavy, I nearly topple over into it head-first from my frantic momentum.

If I don't pick up the pace—and Kane doesn't arrive soon—frostbite will surely begin to set in. My legs are already numb from the wind and beneath my jacket, I'm shivering. I should have put more clothes on. It was stupid not to, but I can't help the tingle that runs through my core as I think about Kane's reaction to seeing me in this ridiculous lingerie, while secretly hoping it sends him into some sex-crazed reaction.

I trudge through the snow as quickly as I can. It's been a solid fifteen minutes since I left the warmth of the house to venture out in my lingerie during an active blizzard. I must be delusional because I feel completely unaffected. My brain is swirling with thoughts of one thing and one thing only, and I've honestly never been so obsessed with an idea like this. The loud rumble of the engine closing in on me snaps me from my sinful thoughts. I scan the white blowing snow, looking for signs of him and spot headlights not far from me. *Thank fuck.* I can't feel my fingers and I'm exhausted from moving through the deep snow, battling the wind, and fighting off thoughts of a serial killer murdering me just like the deer. A small voice dares to question my rationale, urging me to consider if I am truly running to safety or into the arms of danger. *How do I know Kane isn't the serial killer?*

No. Kane can't be a serial killer. This must be death settling into my bones and making my mind delusional. Kane is far too sweet to be a killer. At least I think he is, but then again, how much do I actually know about him?

All around me, the world spins to the point it feels like I'm in the middle of a winter-themed club. The whirling snow pulses to the beat of my heart, and I'm so... alive. *Is this what freezing to death feels like?* I wonder, collapsing into the snow and not realizing it until a pair of thick gloved hands pick me up.

I blink my eyes. "Kane?" I ask in a whisper.

The man who picks me up is wearing a ski mask and goggles. He pulls me into him and all I can feel is the sensation that I'm pressed against him. My body is completely numb.

"Hazel," I can hear him saying. "Why aren't you wearing any clothes?"

I try to answer, but my teeth are chattering. He presses a gloved finger to my lips.

"Shh. Don't talk. We need to get you warmed up." He carries me over to where he left the ATV running when he jumped off it.

He loads us both on, positioning me so my legs straddle over him. He takes off my jacket gently and I try to stop him.

"You need to be warmer. Let me help you." He reaches around us, covering my legs with the jacket, then zips me into him. His chest feels bare beneath his jacket. When my cold body lands against him, Kane flinches.

The next thing I know, he's kissing me, mumbling about how he's so glad I am safe. To my surprise, I kiss him back. His lips are soft and inviting as his tongue slips inside my mouth. I've never been so turned on before. This man wants me and I think I want to know what that feels like. I'm more than along for the ride, enjoying the way he controls our kiss. Until he breaks it.

"Hold on to me." He growls. It's the only warning I get before he shifts into gear and takes off.

I close my eyes, clinging to Kane. My head still feels woozy, but feeling is returning to parts of my body. As soon as I can feel my boobs again, I realize as my body slides against his that he's wearing a thermal shirt. Which also explains why he felt so warm when I fell against him.

My hard nipples press against him and I swear I hear his breath catch, but that would be impossible over the roar of the engine and the whistling wind. There's no time to think about it. The machine grinds to a halt rather suddenly, and then he's lifting me. Kane's carrying me somewhere. At least I think it's Kane. I look up, daring to peek one eye open and scream.

A man in a ski mask stares back at me. He winks, and I'm not sure what to make of it.

"K...K...K. Kane, is that you?" I whisper through chattering teeth.

But he doesn't reply.

Chapter 15

Hazel is fucking terrified. I'm relishing in the fear radiating from her body. It turns me on so much when they get this way, but I promised myself I would keep Hazel alive. I can't respond to her. Can't look at her. Nothing. Not if I want to overcome the intense urge to really play with her. I can feel my grip on reality slipping away. She's all drugged up and high on the love drug. If I want one last huzzah, then I guess this is the one chance I have. I just don't know if I can trust myself not to go too far.

Right now I have two choices: either go ahead with the original plan, tweaking things for an extra good time and hopefully get it out of my system for good, or stick to the boring ass plan.

I spot the dead deer on the back porch right where I left it for her. I get an idea. *Yup, buddy, you win. We are going to do some fucked up things and hope that we don't accidentally fuck up.* My dick flexes in approval. But with a change in plans, I'm going to need some time and a place to relocate the carcass. *The sunroom.* Of course, there's a set of French doors and I can leave Hazel by the fireplace with cookies and some cocoa to get warm. She's probably close to coming down from her first high and in order to avoid a crash, she's going to need a boost. Especially with what I'm planning for us.

I carry Hazel back through her uncle's office and to the sunroom, where I drop her on the oversized loveseat and build a fire. She's definitely going to crash if I don't bump her another cum cookie soon. My cock is straining hard against my pants. Just knowing she's eating my cum gets me so turned on. I hurry to the kitchen and retrieve the plate of cookies. There's still three left. I grab a mug, pour milk into it and pop it in the microwave. Once I've set Hazel up with cookies, cocoa, and music, I step away to deal with the deer. There's a shed below the deck with all the tools I'll need. I head down to Dexter's shed to gather what I need to carve the carcass open and gut the deer. *Santa is going to have such a good time fucking his naughty little reindeer*

I'm a damn serial killer. Of course I'm into some fucked up shit. I work quickly gutting the creature and I don't do a very clean job of it. According to all my tracking, Tyler got on a plane headed back to Colorado this morning, so I know he's well on his way. His flight into Aspen was re-routed to Denver. His bank account information shows he rented a car and obviously intends to come up here. I warned him if he didn't walk away, I would kill him. He should have listened. He should have stayed in Florida.

I heave the carcass across the deck and over to the doors to wait for me. Time to go fuck me a naughty little reindeer. The unhinged part of me I try to keep tucked away is begging to be let free—and knowing that Tyler could potentially walk in on the entire scene only fuels my dubious plans. Carving the carcass was a good buffer between my anger over Tyler and everything I intend to do with Hazel. My mind feels calmer now and I've had time to process, thinking over every last detail.

I hurry back inside to clean my hands up, deciding it's more aesthetic to keep my bloody clothing on. Hazel should be nice and high. Down the hall I slink, all the while getting harder and harder thinking about what it's going to feel like to fuck my girl for the first time. Even if she doesn't realize the serial killer and I are the same person... yet.

When I creep around the corner and into the sunroom, I spot Hazel dancing along to the music in the skimpy little reindeer lingerie I left earlier. It's exactly the confirmation I need to know the drugs are in full effect. She's all loosened up and ready to go. My cock strains against my pants and I can feel the pre-cum leaking out from my excitement. She's so goddamn sexy. *I can't wait to break her.* Hazel does a twirl, flipping her hair and shaking her ass a little to the beat. *Fuck.* When she bends over, she's facing away from me and that short leather skirt rides up her thick thighs, giving me a quick view of her perfect pink pussy falling out of the itty bitty lace thong. I drop my jacket on the ground and strip off my shirt until I'm standing in only my thermal blood-stained pants and boots. My hand slides over my cock to grip it and then I stroke myself from the base to the tip, accidentally moaning as I do.

Hazel twirls around to face me with a gasp, then smiles.

"Hello, there," she purrs. "Are you the big bad serial killer here to hurt me?" She asks, tilting her head to one side with a giggle.

"Mmmm." I groan as her big round tits bounce with her movement.

"You could take your mask off and stay awhile instead. I'm awfully lonely. I just broke up with my boyfriend and the guy who got me this outfit totally ghosted me. Unless you killed him? No matter, you're here now." She licks her lips.

This is going to be more fun than I thought. I had no idea my girl was such a little slut. My anger bubbles and I have to remind stalker me that Kane is also one of our personalities. Okay, *fine, one of our main personalities.* It doesn't mean I can't punish her for being so easy, though.

"Hello there, Tempy," I rasp, taking a step toward her to gauge her reaction.

She doesn't seem affected by my advance. Instead, she zeros in on what I called her. Giggling, she says, "My name's not Tempy, silly."

"Sure it is." I wink, taking another step toward Hazel.

"No," she responds more firmly. "Actually, it's not. My name is Hazel."

"Whatever you say, darling."

"Stop that."

"Stop what?" I ask in a teasing tone. I'm not actually doing anything other than inching closer to her so I can wrap my hands around—

She interrupts my thoughts, "Stop calling me Tempy. Why are you doing that?"

"I wish I could, but I can't because, darling, you're fucking tempting and I intend to enjoy myself."

She giggles, moving her hips in a sexy shimmy. "What should I call you?"

"Santa." I reply.

"But you aren't Santa. You're the serial killer, aren't you?" She asks.

I've distracted Hazel enough to be only a few steps away from her as I gaze at her relentlessly. Her body fills out the skimpy lingerie in all the right places. She's got me so turned on, I can feel my cock throbbing, just aching to be inside that tight pussy. Realizing I'm not saying anything else, she goes back to dancing. Spinning around and looking back over her shoulder at me with a seductive smile.

I get the feeling all these sexy dance moves are just for me, and I'm not complaining one bit. When I can't stand to watch her any longer, I clear the space between us, pulling her against me. I know she can feel my dick as she grinds momentarily on me

Hazel yelps in surprise as if she's completely forgotten I'm here at all. Her hands land against my chest inadvertently while I allow mine to wander her body, running them over her soft, supple skin. She leans into me closer, throwing her head back with a soft moan.

"That's it, darling. Let me know you like it." I groan.

"Mmmm. Mister big, bad serial killer, you can touch me anywhere you want. Because I *do* like it," she whispers seductively.

"Deal," I growl.

Chapter 16

Hazel has no idea the beast she awoke when she whispered those words. I want to touch her so many places, and with her permission I stop holding back. My fingers trail over her curves, roughly ravishing her body and reveling in the way it responds to me. She's grinding into me and I can feel the heat from her arousal against my cock. I groan, gripping her by the hair, then bringing her close enough to whisper in her ear.

"Do you know how much I am enjoying this?" I pant.

She giggles, but doesn't answer.

It doesn't matter, I'm going to lose control. Her nipples brush against my chest as she leans in close. She feels so good, I drag my thumb across one nipple, taking care to tease her until she pulls away from the irritation. *I need more.* I drop my hand to hold her by one hip, dipping my other beneath her skimpy leather skirt.

"You're fucking soaked, little reindeer," I rasp heavily, running my fingers over her wet panties one more time.

She moans, pressing against my fingertips as if she's begging for me to slip inside.

"What is it, darling? Use your words. Tell Santa what you want."

"More." Hazel begs.

"More what? Be a good little reindeer and tell me, darling. Do you want me to make you cum?"

She places her hands so she's cupping my jaw through the mask and looks at me, her green eyes sparkling. "Yes, Santa. Please make me cum."

I hold her gaze and watch her eyes widen as I slip my finger beneath her panties, dragging them through her folds, spreading her wetness. I give her clit a swirl and she hisses with delight, then I slip my finger inside her hot pussy, curling it while my thumb works her swollen clit.

"Let's play Santa says, Hazel."

"Whatever you say, Santa," she winks.

This girl is way too much fun when she's high. She really is the woman of my dreams—knowing I get to keep her all to myself only makes me enjoy this more. It only takes a few strokes before she's losing herself to my movements, tilting her hips in rhythm with me. She's getting wobbly and her walls are closing around my finger. I slip a second one inside and give her the web slinger motion, coaxing out her orgasm before growling, "Santa says cum."

No sooner do the words roll off my tongue and she's coating me in her release. My cock is swollen and hard. If she were to grind against it right now, I would probably come. Good thing I prepped with a certain little fun-time pill. I'm going to be fucking her until she can't walk.

Tyler must have a tiny dick because she's as tight as a virgin. I'm going to be stretching her out to accommodate me. Pre-cum leaks out at the thought and my dick throbs, aching to be inside her. I need to calm down so I don't come, or maybe coming a little is exactly what I need to do to relieve some of the pressure building in my balls.

"Good, little reindeer," I praise. "Let's play again."

She smiles at me, moving her body to the music seductively. Who knew dancing to Christmas music could be so goddamn sexy. "Say *yes Santa.*"

"Yes, Santa," she purrs.

"Santa says: Get on your knees, little reindeer, and suck this dick like a good girl."

She drops to the ground at my feet, waiting for me to release my bulging cock from beneath my pants. Either she's too high to notice the blood, or she doesn't care. I personally think she's rolling hard. My eyes dart to the small table where I left the plate of cookies. *She ate them all.* This is going to be so much fun.

She clears her throat, eyeing my cock as I pull it out, watching as her eyes bulge. I grip it at the base, stroking my hand over myself slowly. Hazel parts her mouth while her gaze is locked on mine and I place the head against her lips. She licks just my tip in a painfully slow motion, then swirls her tongue around me and sucks just my tip into her hot mouth. It feels incredible as she pops me in and out. I want to be deeper. I want to feel her throat constricting around me as she gags. This next time, when she sucks me back into her mouth, I press my dick in deeper, thrusting my hips forward. Her jaw stretched open further to accommodate me. I love the way her lips are wrapped around me. I slide myself out a little, watching as she leaves a trail of saliva behind. Then I thrust in further, making her take more of me. Her nostrils flail as she tries to suck in a breath. I pull out, relishing in the sound as she gasps for air before dragging her tongue over my length and swirling it around my head again.

"You're doing such a good job," I moan.

She looks up at me, smiles, then sucks me into her mouth, swallowing more of my length until she has every last inch inside her mouth. She swallows, her throat constricting around my throbbing dick. My cum is leaking out. I feel so full.

"Santa says: Let me fuck those pretty lips until I cum down your throat and, Hazel, you better swallow every last drop." I close my eyes and begin rhythmically fucking her mouth.

My orgasm builds. I'm so close and then I feel her tongue press up and against the bottom of me. The sensation sends me over the edge and I grab Hazel by the hair holding her in place, forcing her to choke on the cum exploding down her throat.

"That's it, darling, swallow Santa's cum." There's so much, it drips out the side of her mouth, mixing with saliva.

She's fucking perfect. If only we could reach a point in our relationship where we can do this kind of shit without drugs. I look at her, tilting my head to one side, considering it. *Can she love me?* I pull my cock free, wiping my cum from the corner of her mouth, then pressing my fingers into her mouth. "Every last drop, darling"

"Hazel." My voice is husky and ragged, my cock still hard and pulsing. "I want to play another round. Do you want to keep playing with me?" I pinch her nipple, rolling it between my fingers.

Hazel licks her lips, swiping her tongue across them, then sucking her bottom lip in. "I want to play again."

"Tell me, beautiful, do you want Santa to stretch that pussy out so you can take me?" I pull her off her knees so she's standing.

My greedy fingers find the elastic band of her thong and I hook them around it, sliding her drenched panties down her thick thighs. I want so badly to run my tongue over the trail to taste her sweet juices. *I bet she tastes fucking amazing.* But my vision is blurring and I can feel the thrill of the hunt pulling at the edges of the last bit of my control. My primal instincts threaten to consume me, but I fight it off. *I don't want to break this toy.* My hand slips over her bare pussy, cupping it, before I drag my fingers through her folds. She moans and writhes against me. Her wetness coats my fingers and I bring them to my lips to taste her. *Just one taste.*

The taste of her cum on my tongue sends me somewhere dark and a small thread of my control snaps. I'm barely holding it together. I slide my other hand around her neck as she looks into my eyes; the fear returning to hers. Fuck. I feel the last bit of restraint snap.

"Santa says: Be my good little reindeer, darling, and run." My words come out in a guttural snarl and Hazel turns, bolting from me—right toward the French doors where the carcass waits for her on the other side.

I take a few long strides and then she screams. I'm right behind her, though, snatching her by the hair and shoving her into the carcass. "That's a good girl. Climb inside and let Santa stretch that pussy out."

I shove her until she's on her hands and knees as if she's going to wear the carcass, then give her ass a slap, watching as it jiggles. My hand leaves a red print on her perfect ass. I want to be inside her, but I want to enjoy it. I look around and consider my options, admiring the way her pink little pussy peeks out from under the skirt, tempting me. *I'll use my fingers first,* I decide, dropping to my knees. I pop my fingers in my mouth to wet them with saliva, then thrust them into her, playing with her clit while I work Hazel up to take me. She rocks back and forth, riding my fingers until she comes undone on them.

My cock flexes. I'm getting hard enough to fuck her again, but she's not ready yet. I let her catch her breath and look around. It's freezing cold outside, and the snow is coming down. My dick isn't going to stay hard in the weather. I have to make the choice to drag the carcass inside. I pull my fingers from her pussy, immediately missing the way it was still pulsing around them.

"Roll over, little reindeer, so I can fill you up." She hesitates, looking over her shoulder wearily.

"It will keep you warm while I fill you, darling. Don't you want Santa to fill you up?" I ask her, keeping my voice smooth and even-toned, even though her defiance is making my blood boil.

Hazel takes another moment, thinking it over, then twists around slowly, leaning back into the open carcass. She truly looks as if she's some kind of reindeer skinwalker as she lays inside the carcass, wearing the deer waiting for me to keep my promise and fill her up. She bites her bottom lip, looking up at me. "Fill me up. I need to feel you."

I drag the carcass into the sunroom and growl, "Not yet. Your pussy isn't ready for me."

She sulks, and then my eyes land on it. There's a decent-sized thick icicle hanging from the deck rail a few feet from me. I tuck my dick into my pants, protecting it from the snow blowing outside, and walk over to break it off. I watch Hazel from the corner of my eye. She doesn't move a muscle. When I return, I brandish the big thick icicle in front of her. For a moment I imagine ramming it through her body and using it to hold her in place while I fuck her—then I remember how much I want to keep her alive, at least long enough to make Tyler watch me fuck her.

"You shouldn't be such a dirty little slut, darling. You didn't listen." I say, finding my self-control.

"You didn't say *Santa says.*" She quips.

"Well now, I'm going to fuck you with this icicle until you're too numb to feel my dick inside you. Santa says: Open your legs." I slam the doors closed and lock them as she swallows a lump in her throat with a gulp.

I'm about to take temperature play to another level.

Hazel

Chapter 17

I t's freezing cold. I don't understand how his dick can feel cold and hard. Everything is so wet as he pumps in and out of me. Suddenly I'm empty and then I feel something warm and moist wrap around my clit. The warmth is painful in the most delightful way, as it shocks the cold his cock left behind. I squeal, overcome with pleasure at the way pressure is building in my clit. It feels like I'm going to come, but my core is still numb. *What did Sexy Santa say earlier about a punishment?* I try to remember, but I think I was too busy staring at his giant bulge. I can feel the soft, distant pull of my orgasm building. It sends me into a blissful haze. My eyes squeeze closed and a primal moan escapes my lips.

"That's it, my naughty little reindeer. Tell Santa how good he makes you feel." The masked man says.

"Sexy Santa," I say unfiltered, "You make me feel so good. Your dick is so cold and hard."

He laughs and so do I. I don't know why we are laughing, but the masked man's laugh turns maniacal and I immediately stop laughing.

"That's adorable, Hazel."

The way he says my name is intoxicating. I immediately want him to say it again. "Hmmm," I giggle, flirting with him.

He smiles down at me, his perfect teeth are as white as snow. His lips are full in all the right places and his eyes, they glint with a dangerous darkness that only makes him irresistible. My sudden attraction to him is insatiable. I want him to watch me; I want him to touch me. More than anything, though, I want him to fuck me hard with that enormous cock of his.

"That wasn't my cock, darling. When I stuff this big dick into that tight little pussy, you'll know, and you'll beg me to destroy you." He rasps in a husky tone, filled deep with need.

"Then what was it you stuffed me with, Sexy Santa?" I ask, genuinely interested in knowing.

He holds up a very large icicle, its as thick in diameter as Tyler's dick. He was fucking me with an icicle. *Masked Santa is kinky. I hope I'm not dreaming because, fuck, I want him to be real.* I try to think of the last thing I remember, but if this is a dream, it's not one of those where you can manipulate the storyline. I'm left to question if any of this is real.

"Should I do it again, and get you nice and numb so I can slide my dick inside? Are you ready to take Santa's big dick, darling?" He asks.

Unashamed at how good an icicle felt, I nod my head *yes* eagerly.

"What's that, Hazel? Remember, you need to use your words, or I'll be forced to withhold your orgasms from you." He means every word of it.

I correct myself and purr, "I want you to fuck me with the icicle, please."

"Look at you, begging so good," his deep voice rumbles. "How about I eat that pussy while I fuck you with the icicle?"

He doesn't wait for my answer. "Yes, please San—" Is all I can get out before his mouth encircles my clit.

His tongue dipping into my entrance, tasting me, then pulling away. Only for the warmth of his mouth to be replaced with the shocking cold of the icicle sliding thick side first into me. I groan, opening my legs, longing to feel his mouth on me. As if on cue, his warm soft tongue glides over my clit, sending waves of pleasure through me. I can feel my pussy clenching the icicle. The heat from my core is melting it, making things extra wet.

Sexy Masked Santa fucks me with an icicle while licking and sucking my pussy until I come hard everywhere and then he tosses it to the side, steps out of his boots, removes his pants and surrounds me with his body. His arms land around the deer I'm laying in and his body covers mine. He drops to an elbow while still maintaining eye contact, then reaches down with one hand to slide my knee open wider, positioning me in a way where my hips are wide open and ready to accommodate him.

I can't feel anything but cold and numbness for a minute, but then I feel the pressure of his head pressing against my entrance. It's just as big as I thought it would feel. He's never going to fit inside of me.

"Relax, my naughty little reindeer, let me fill you up and pump you full of Santa's seed."

Once again, he doesn't wait for my response. He rams into my pussy in one hard thrust. I feel pain at first but it's more of an uncomfortable feeling. His cock is just as hard as the icicle, but it's burning hot and pulsating inside me like a vibrator as it rams in and out. One. Two. Three more passes, and I'm coming. My hot cum thaws my frozen core, sending a sharp rush of pain through me as he switches arms. Reaching down between my legs to stroke my clit, he pounds into me.

I've never felt anything like this before. The sensation of being stuffed so full that my pussy feels as if it might burst is amazing. I've never felt this kind of full and I don't want it to end. My eyes squeeze tighter as he builds another orgasm up, before sending its waves washing over me again. This time I only squirt a little but it's enough for him to hiss, "Oh-my-fucking-god."

He's going to cum. I can feel him getting harder and longer inside of me, and it makes my pussy feel as if it's being torn open at the seams. He pumps me harder and faster. My toes are curling, my back arching—then when I think I can experience no more pleasure, his hot cum shoots deep inside of me, filling my pussy full of him. I come again, my walls squeezing every drop of cum from his spent cock.

I scream for him. "Yes, Santa. Please, Santa. Oh my god!"

Kane

Chapter 18

She's spent and satiated. It feels so good. I leave my dick inside her until I feel it go all the way soft. We are both breathing heavily. I couldn't have fantasized anything better than what the two of us just did. If only she knew her Sexy Santa and Kane are both the same person.

As much as I want to run into Tyler, the fact I'm exhausted and Hazel is due to come down hard anytime now means it's probably time to grab a few things for her, bundle up, and head out. *What are you doing, Kane?* I ask myself.

I'm taking her home. We can clean her up and play with her again while we wait for Tyler. It's not a bad idea. She's going to sleep forever. I want to be well rested for when I get to come face to face with Tyler. He may try to confess to everything that happened—the deal I made him—but I know I can manipulate Hazel into believing he's just trying to blame an innocent stranger. Play it off as if he can't stand to see her with someone who can actually take care of her.

Tyler really should have stayed in Florida. *He's going to regret this.* I check my watch. Once I clean us both up, I'll find out where Tyler is and why he hasn't arrived yet. He missed a good show and I'm a little disappointed about it.

In the carcass, Hazel is about to drift off. I leave her there and go to the bedroom to grab one of her duffle bags to pack a few things for her. I'm going to scatter everything else over the bedroom and down the hall. Tyler won't know what to think. I smile malevolently. This is shaping up to be the best Christmas ever. I work quickly, not wanting Tyler to arrive and catch me off guard. I only hope that the pass was closed on the mountain and he's stuck somewhere until they get the road cleared in the morning. The blizzard hasn't let up at all. The roads have to be impossible to drive through at night. I'm not going to wait and find out.

I put out the fire in the family room, then go in search of Hazel's jacket, winter gear, and find her clothes from earlier. I leave the clothes and snag the winter gear. I pulled a pair of sweatpants and a sweatshirt for her to wear on the ride back. *It's going to suck getting her down to the ATV.* When I return to Hazel, she's dozing with her eyes closed, but they flutter open when she hears my footsteps.

"Let's get you dressed and to bed." I pull her from the carcass, stripping her lingerie off and leaving it for Tyler to find.

I dress her, bundling us both up, put out the burning embers in the sunroom, then carry her and the duffle bag through all the snow to the ATV. I'm hot and sweaty by the time I get to it and looking forward to the cold wind whipping around me.

I shouldn't be bringing her back to my place. Nothing good ever happens there—the last thing I need is for her to wander into my office and find all my research on her. There's also the basement. I'll need to lock it up so she doesn't accidentally stumble upon my museum before I'm ready for her to see it. *This is a bad idea and I know it, but I want her in my bed with me tonight.* I want to press my hard cock against her and wake up with her in my arms. She'll probably sleep for an entire day. I'm only going to sleep for a few hours to recharge. Then I need to get my eyes on Tyler and his progress. I want to know when I should expect him so I can prepare for his arrival properly.

The wind blows in gusts, threatening to send us both falling into the snow banks accumulating everywhere. When I finally reach the ATV, I set Hazel on the seat and start it up so it can warm. I can't run it on a cold engine. While it idles, I kick out the snow from around my tires and strap Hazel's bag down with bungee cords. I look at Hazel. She's shivering, slumped over, barely able to keep her eyes open. The sun is setting, so the little sunlight and warmth it was providing are fading quickly. I spin Hazel around so she can cling onto me while I drive, then climb on and help her drape her legs over mine. She wraps them around my waist, squeezing me tightly. I pull her closer and whisper, "Hold on."

The snow is blowing in the same direction we are traveling, which makes the drive tolerable and easy. I should really plow, but I think I'll hold off until morning just to make sure Tyler doesn't come poking around tonight. The terrain is too steep, and the snow makes the trail slick. It's a good thing I have snow chains on to grip into it and propel us up my long driveway. We arrive and Hazel is still fighting to keep her eyes open. "Let me get you all cleaned up and into bed." She nods. I close the garage and grab her bag, tossing it over my shoulder before I pick up the girl of my dreams and carry her into what I hope can one day be our home. Hazel rests her head against my chest in exhaustion and I lightly kiss the top of her head, but I don't think she notices.

Inside, I carry her to my quarters so I can clean us up and tuck her into bed. Depositing her on the floor, I turn on the shower and prepare everything I need to bathe her in my special soaps. *One of my personalities obviously intended to bring her home, even though we all know it's a terrible plan.*

Once the shower is ready, I strip us both down, removing the mask and stashing it away. I doubt she'll remember much from today, but it's always best to play things safe. I help a very groggy Hazel to the shower. The next time I plan this, I'll give her a bath. I'm tired from fucking her, and it's a lot of work to keep her steady. Despite my fatigue, I still enjoy washing every inch of her. All the while, she keeps moaning and sighing as I massage and wash her body. I hold onto her with one hand, then clean myself with my own soap. When we finish, I dress her in the flannel snowman pajamas I packed her. Hazel leans against me while I brush her hair out so it's not a tangled mess in the morning. I braid it for her, reminiscent to how I used to for my mother when she started having bad days from the treatment. I finish and tuck her into my bed, standing back to admire the way she looks all curled up safe and sound in it. If she knew about the monster inside of me, I doubt she'd sleep so peacefully. Soon I'll find out, though. I'll see if she can love me back. I creep away to lock up the basement and the office, but before I lock it up, I plan to find out where Tyler is. Once I know, I'll climb into bed with my girl and fall asleep with her in my arms, enjoying the smell of my cum covering her body.

Chapter 19

Six hours later, I'm dressed in a pair of gray sweatpants and an unbuttoned green and black flannel shirt, strolling through the kitchen with a cup of coffee in hand as I head to my office. It's time to check on Tyler and the road closures. Last night he had to stop on the other side of the pass and get a hotel. I unlock the door, silently slipping inside. It's not likely Hazel will wake up any time soon but I have motion detecting cameras set up all over the house to let me know if she does. My fingers slide over the keys, typing in my password. Once I have everything loaded, I dig for updates. The hotel is first. I open his email searching for a generic 'thank you for your stay' check-out email and notice it's time stamped for just after five-thirty AM. That was an hour ago. If the pass is open, he's still at least three hours out because climbing the mountain will require snow chains on his tires. He's not as dumb as I thought. Unfortunately, he made sure to rent a car with four-wheel drive. *He's actually pretty stupid leaving the nice life we set up for him in Florida.* Instead of living near the beach, he'll be living in my basement, stuffed and perfectly preserved, another body to add to the collection. My fingers whirl over the keyboard, pausing only to click around with the mouse. I hack into the hotel's cameras and watch the security footage of him leaving, and then log in to check his bank account for gas station charges. When I finish my deep-dive, I'm estimating Tyler will arrive at Hazel's in the next hour and a half or so, depending on how skilled of a driver he is and if he can even make it through the roads leading up here.

I check my cameras at Hazel's, making sure all the motion detectors are turned on, then wander out of the office, locking the door behind me. I want everything to be perfect for her. Looking around, there are Christmas decorations everywhere, filling every space with holiday magic. I can't wait for her to wake up and see how perfect this place is. While I wait, I guess I can bake her some gingerbread cookies for a change in desserts. The royal icing piped around the cookie decoratively will be the perfect place for me to hide my secret ingredients. We can even share with Tyler. My chuckling cascades through the silence. It will be fun to play with Tyler. Since he's sacrificing himself, I'll still have a body for this year. I haven't missed a Christmas since I started, but I think I would give it all up for Hazel. At least the keeping them part. There are a few like Tyler. I'm not sure I would be willing to dispose of right away, but eventually maybe I could be convinced to get rid of them all. I sigh, a weight lifting from my shoulders. I've been so worried about bringing Hazel here—and trying to keep her alive—but knowing I get to watch her murder the man she loves and surrender herself to me completely has the dull ache to kill Hazel cured. Come to think of it, I no longer feel the need to harm her. If she can give herself to me fully like that—well, I'll never find another woman like her. She's perfect for me.

I get to work on the cookies. If I can replicate the effects of the last batch, then I know I can get Hazel to do anything I want. And I want my sweet little Jane Doe to kill Tyler while making him watch me fuck his girl like the dirty little slut she is. Hazel needs a man like me, someone built with the ability to satisfy her sexual needs and fantasies. I can't wait to bury my cock in her tight little pussy over and over again for the rest of my life, just the way it was always meant to be. She's mine. Hazel belongs to me now and no other cock will ever be able to stretch her out and satisfy her the way mine can. Especially not Tyler. That little pencil dick is going to watch her take a real man while I work her over, pleasuring her in ways he'll never have the chance to.

While the cookies bake, I check on Hazel. When I find her still crashed hard, I slip out of my room, closing the door softly behind me and return to the garage, where I start the truck and let it warm up so I can plow. I've changed my mind. Rather than prevent Tyler from coming here, I want him delivered to my doorstep, so I can rub it all in his stupid face before I take him down to Hazel's, tie him up and let him sleep off some Ambien. I'll have to let the cookies cool before I can frost them, and plowing will give me more time to think and plan. My timer dings for the cookies and I grab an oven mitt, pulling the trays from the oven so this batch can cool.

Next time I can bring Hazel into the kitchen to bake with me and we can have an extra good time. Desperate to be with her again, I let my thoughts drift off, imagining all the ways I could fuck her in the kitchen. First, I picture her in nothing but an apron, her tits flashing me as they fall out from behind the fabric, and her pussy inviting me to slip inside while bending her over the counter and feeding Hazel a warm fresh-baked cookie. I groan, realizing I'm stroking myself and shrug, grabbing a cup to come in. *Only the fresh stuff for my girl.* Squeezing my eyes shut, I let the scene play out. I'm pumping into her and she's taking every inch of me while she begs me to fill her. I moan, then open my eyes just in time to make sure I get it all in the cup just as I come. Then I cover it with a bit of plastic wrap and leave it hidden in the pantry for later. I don't want Hazel to come downstairs and find it while I'm out. Better to be safe than sorry.

The truck should be nice and warmed up so I slip on my boots and head out to clear Tyler a path to death's doorstep.

Kane

Chapter 20

The plowing is done, cookies are frosted, a fire is crackling, and above me, Hazel is sleeping all curled up in bed. Tyler arrived at Hazel's an hour ago. He ran around in a panic and I watched with delight. He's on his way here now and I can't wait for him to ring the doorbell. I've been watching the front cameras diligently, waiting for him to arrive. I prepared an Ambien cocoa for him and all it needs is a quick ride in the microwave.

The wood floor creaks beneath my feet as I pace the room, watching and waiting. Finally, I hear a knock on the front door. It's time. I can't fucking wait to kill Tyler with the love of my life wrapped around my dick. I smile wickedly for a moment then swing the door open to stand face to face with Tyler, except he doesn't know I'm me... yet.

Tyler is short, maybe five-foot-ten. He's a scrawny guy with not much meat on his bones and it doesn't look like he's ever been to a gym. I'm not sure what Hazel saw in him. He's average looking. There's nothing special about him. *She must have liked him for his personality. Yuck!* I try not to let my face show the disgust I'm feeling.

"Are you okay, sir? Do you need help?" I ask, innocently.

He gawks at me, unable to speak for a moment. *I tend to have that effect on people.*

When he finds his voice, he stammers, "I'm sorry to bother you, but I came up here to visit my girlfriend and surprise her for Christmas Eve. When I got there, the back door on the patio was broken. There's a deer with its inside parts all over the back deck. Hazel's things were everywhere, but she's nowhere to be found." His voice is distressed as he describes all the surprises I left for him.

"Ex-girlfriend," I mutter.

"What?" Tyler asks, confusion covering his face.

"Oh, it's just I could have sworn when Hazel came up here, all distressed, she mentioned a crazy ex-boyfriend who she thought was trying to chase after her." I keep my tone even and calm.

"Wait, is Hazel here?" He asks.

"That depends," I say, crossing my arms.

"I fail to see how it depends. Is my girlfriend here or not?" Tyler asks gruffly.

"Ex-girlfriend," I repeat.

"Why don't you come inside and warm up? You can tell me what's going on." I coax, opening the door.

He looks at me, weighing whether it's an invitation or a demand, then finally steps inside. "Yeah, sure, why not?"

Good boy

I place my hand on his shoulder and give it a squeeze, leading him into the living room where the fire is crackling and Christmas movie is playing on the TV.

"Grab a seat and I'll bring us some cocoa. Is peppermint okay?"

"Uh, sure," he says nervously.

I give him an unnerving smile, then go to the kitchen to retrieve the mug I prepared for him earlier. Once it's warm, I give it a stir and top it with whipped cream and crushed candy cane. I take it out to him, then make myself a cup. When I return, I sit down across from him on the edge of the sectional and take a sip.

"Start from the beginning," I say.

"This is going to sound insane, but here it goes." Tyler takes a few drinks of cocoa and a deep breath. "About a month ago, a man called me. He didn't say who he was. All he said was he would pay me a lot of money if I left Colorado—and Hazel—behind. He had a lot of demands about how he wanted things to go down and he offered to pay me a lot of money. More money than I could ever imagine. I'm not broke. I make a decent living, but these amounts were life-changing. Before you judge me for taking the money, there was one more thing. He told me if I didn't go willingly, he would have no choice but to take me out. This guy threatened to kill me, so I did exactly what he told me to." Tyler pauses to take a few more drinks of cocoa.

"Please continue. What happened after you took the money and disappeared?" I ask.

"Why does it matter? Why am I even telling you this?" Tyler breaks down, looking at me suspiciously.

"You're telling me because I know where Hazel is, and what she told me and the sheriff," his eyes bulge when I mention the sheriff.

"The sheriff?" He squawks.

"Yes. From what she's mentioned, it was a really nasty breakup and her ex, presumably you, are some kind of a twisted psychopath. So now you see why I need to hear your side of the story before I decide to tell you where she is."

He rolls his eyes, clearly upset over having been made the villain, but eager enough to prove his innocence that he continues on with his confession.

"I got to Florida and let things cool down. It seemed like this guy just disappeared and I've been missing Hazel. I was planning to propose to her. I've been paying off a ring and I was going to surprise her during our anniversary trip to Mexico. So I booked a plane ticket and rented a car to come up here because her parents said she came up here to clear her head after our breakup." He drains his cup of cocoa.

I take a sip of mine and smile at him. His eyes are looking heavy and he shifts uncomfortably.

"Something wrong, mister—"

"Tyler," he interjects, reaching his hand out to shake mine, but I'm sitting across the rug from him and I don't move to accept it, so he drops it awkwardly.

"Are you feeling okay, Tyler?" I ask.

"Mph," he grunts. "I'm just jet-lagged and tired from driving all day in the snowstorm. It's nothing."

I nod. "Well that's quite the story, Tyler. Hazel told it a lot differently."

"Yeah," Tyler replies, his eyelids drooping as he fights to stay awake. "Where's Hazel? You never answered me."

"My apologies, Tyler, I'm still assessing whether or not you deserve to know where she is." I reply curtly.

"Why do you get to decide if I see her or not?" Agitation lacing his words with fire.

I tsk my tongue at him. "Now, now, now, Tyler. Is that anyway to speak to your gracious host?"

His face contorts with fury. "Gracious," he whisper-shouts through his overwhelming grogginess.

I nod my head. "I've been a very gracious host, Tyler, and very tolerant of you. I called you politely to inform you of my intentions. I entertained your negotiations and requests for a house closer to the beach. Most importantly, Tyler, I've offered to spare your life, and yet here we sit. You're in my living room demanding to see your ex-girlfriend and I've been quite tolerable about all of this right up until you confessed you intended to go back on our bargain."

He slowly puts it all together and his lips barely fall open in shock. He's trying so hard to keep his eyes open.

"You!" He slurs. "Give me Hazel back."

"Oh, don't worry about that, Tyler. She's tucked in my bed, nice and safe, sleeping." I reply, my smile spreading from ear to ear as his head falls forward, and he jerks it up, trying to stay conscious.

"Did you," he pauses, drifting off. "Did you drug me?" Tyler's speech is further slurred.

I walk over and cover him with a blanket, leaning into his face as I do. "Sorry, Tyler, I had to drug you. I told you to disappear and instead you show up on my doorstep to confess your plans to double-cross me."

"What?" Tyler says, rubbing his eyes. "Who are you?"

"I'm probably your worst nightmare, or the equivalent of the Grim Reaper." I taunt. "But for the purpose of sticking to the plan, I'm anonymous and that's all you need to know about me. Now Tyler—"

"Mmmph," he replies.

"Enjoy your nap. When you wake up, I'm going to kill you and it will be agony."

"Worst nightmare." He repeats.

"Yes, Tyler. I'm your worst nightmare and I'm going to keep your girl. The thing is, I'm already in love with her. I saw her first, and judging by the way she was screaming for me a few hours ago, I think she's long moved on from you."

"You're a psychopath," Tyler mumbles.

"Yes, Tyler. I'm a psychopath. I tried to warn you, but you're a fucking idiot who should have never crossed a serial killer. Sleep tight, Tyler, because I'm going to fucking kill you." I hiss.

I walk away, leaving him to his panic. When I return ten minutes later, he's laying on the couch. A snore escapes his lips and I stare at him, unmoving. I set a running stopwatch on my phone and check the time. I'll give him fifteen more minutes before I tie him up and haul him back to Hazel's place. Once she wakes up, we can go visit him and get his untimely death over with so we can live together happily ever after.

Once fifteen minutes passes I do just that. I tie him up securely, place him in my truck, and drive down to Hazel's, depositing him in the living room for later. While I'm there, I turn the heat all the way down to sixty-three. I want him to be uncomfortable. As soon as I finish, I drive back up the road to my place and climb into bed with Hazel, hoping she'll wake up in my arms in the morning.

Hazel

Chapter 21

My eyes flutter open, but nothing looks familiar. I wait for my vision to come into focus and for my brain to catch up. Then scan my surroundings again. I have no idea where I am. A light snore comes from behind me and I jump, only to realize there's a man's arm wrapped around me. For a moment I think it's just Tyler, but then I remember I broke up with Tyler. I yelp. Sitting up straight in bed and scooting away from the devilishly handsome man laying on the pillow next to me.

He opens his eyes and smiles at me. "Look who's finally awake." I stare back at him, confused. My head is pounding, the room is spinning, my lips are dry and hard, and I feel dehydrated. Did I get drunk and fuck Kane? I try to scan my thoughts and remember the last thing I remember doing. None of my memories are of Kane, though. I had a crazy dream about Santa and I think I fucked him, but I'm really not sure because it's all really blurry. Before that, I think harder trying to remember. I was taking pictures in some lingerie. Is that how I got here? Oh god. The last thing I remember was thinking about sexting Kane. I must have and he obviously felt the same way, or how else would I have ended up here?

"What's wrong, darling? You look like you've seen a ghost." Kane says scooting up in bed, revealing his perfectly muscular chest.

Each one of his abs is perfectly defined, chiseled into his body with an undeniable attention to detail. I'm mesmerized as my eyes follow the hard lines slowing into a V below his belly button. The rest of him is hidden beneath the flannel sheets. I can feel him watching me, enjoying his body. It feels wrong, but I can't bring myself to stop either. When I've finally had enough and I can stand our silence no longer, I bring my eyes to meet his. My cheeks flushed with embarrassment.

"Good morning. I'm sorry I woke you."

He smiles at me in return, swinging his arm so I can scoot in against him. I'm not sure what to do hesitating, but also enticed by the prospect of running my fingers over his abs I decide to scoot closer. His arm snakes around me protectively, pulling me closer and leaning over to kiss me on the head.

"Do you remember anything from last night?" He asks, his voice deep and raspy, still with sleep.

I can feel myself turning red. "Will you be upset if I say no?"

He squeezes me. "Of course not. I'm sure it was incredibly traumatizing to watch everything that psycho did. If you've mentally blocked it out, I will spare you from reliving the details. Just know when you're ready to face him, he's tied up at your uncle's place right where we left him."

I fall against him, allowing one hand to land against his chest. His skin is warm and soft as I slide my fingers over it, tracing the muscles I so desperately wanted to touch when I first saw them. If Kane doesn't want to tell me the details, then I'm not sure I want to know, but if I'm going to face

Tyler, then I should probably have the basics, so I know what to say.

"Kane," I whisper.

"Yes, my darling."

The way he says that gives me butterflies. I've never been anyone's darling. "If I asked you to tell me what happened, but without all the details, would you? I don't even know what to say to Tyler."

He sighs. "I don't want to, but I realize you need to know. How much do you remember?"

"I don't think I remember anything," I confess, shifting so I can roll into him, draping one leg over his hip.

Instinctively, his other hand drops over me and he traces the curve of my hip a few times before cupping my face. "If you need me to stop at any point, just squeeze my hand." He holds his hand out to me and I take it, and then he clears his throat.

"You called me and said there was a deer on the deck. It ran into the glass door of the sunroom, and you were panicking." His eyes search my face to make sure I'm okay still. Satisfied, he continues. "I came down right away, but when I got there, you were running through the snow and yelling for help. You told me he was hunting you and if he caught up to you, he would kill you like he had the deer.

You begged me to bring you here because you were too terrified to return to your uncle's house."

My eyes are filled with tears. Tyler came up here to hurt me. How could he? I gave him everything he wanted. I was patient when he said he wasn't ready to get married or settle down. Now I know why he didn't want to, but how could he come here just to harm me after he was the one that left? My head is spinning and I let it fall against Kane's chest while I take a deep breath.

He releases my hand so he can stroke the hair back from my face. "Let's finish this story after breakfast. I knew your morning would be rough, so I made you fresh apple cinnamon and cranberry muffins with walnuts."

I nod, eager for the break and needing time to wrap my head around what happened.

"Kane," I whisper again.

"Yes, my darling."

"Did we?" I'm not able to bring myself to finish the sentence.

He grins down at me. "Yes, and I have no problem reminding you how it went later, but first, you need to eat."

"You want to do it again?" I squeak in surprise.

"If I had my way, we would never stop doing it. Hazel, I think you have me addicted and I never want to spend another moment without you. Holding you in my arms these last few hours has been perfect. I only wish Dex was here, but maybe he brought you to me because he knew we could heal each other." Kane's words overwhelm my emotions and a tear slides down my face.

"Shhh. Come here. Don't cry, Hazel. I promise you I will make up for every year you spent without me. I only want—"

"You only want what?" I ask him.

"Promise you won't laugh?" He asks.

"Promise."

"I was really hoping meeting you would be as perfect as it is, and we could fall in love like in those cheesy holiday movies and have a happily ever after. You see, I've always longed for companionship—someone who could love me for who I am and not the numbers in my bank account. I felt like you were my only hope and now here we are together and I never want this to end." He confesses.

Tears stream down my face uncontrollably. "Kane," I choke on my sob. "I could never laugh. I wanted that, too. In fact, I've been watching holiday romances and wishing I could be one of those lucky girls. When you showed up to shovel my snow, I wanted it to be you."

He wipes my tears with the back of his hand. "It can be Hazel. All you have to do is promise to love me, and in return, I promise to love you more than you ever thought possible. I will give you the world if you can see me for who I am and love me."

I wrap my arms around his neck. *How is this happening?* I pinch my wrist, checking to make sure I'm not dreaming. *Is this really happening? Am I getting a traumatic holiday knight in shining armor love story for Christmas?* I blink in disbelief, squeezing him closer.

"Are you real?" I whisper, so in shock, my filter seems to have disappeared.

"I promise you I am very real, and I am very serious. Come downstairs with me and let me show you around. I love Christmas, and I want you to experience our shared love for the season all over again. Since you don't remember much from last night."

He's perfect. Absolutely perfect. I allow him to pull me from his bed, but then he scoops me up in his arms, carrying me as if I am unable to walk on my own.

"Let me carry you down the stairs. I want to hold you, and I'm not ready to let you go yet."

He doesn't have to ask me twice. I'm sold. I feel like the luckiest girl in the world right now.

When he steps out from the hall and onto the landing, my breath catches. "Oh my god, Kane!" I gush. Fresh-cut garland drenched with poinsettias and soft twinkling lights adorn the railing of his circular staircase. Red velvet ribbons run down the rails, curling at the end. I look up to whisper in his ear. "This is every girl's dream holiday romance movie."

"Why is that, darling?" His nickname for me makes me squirm as I revel in the feel of it.

His smile lifts in the corners of his mouth when he looks down at me, waiting for my reply.

"A mansion, decked out for Christmas, on top of a mountain with snow blowing in the large windows built for enjoying the magnificent views." I giggle.

"And," he prompts me.

"And the most handsome man I think I've ever met, complete with abs that don't look real." I cover my mouth, laughing awkwardly at my overshare.

He stops at the top of the stairs and looks up. "Mistletoe."

My hand guides his face to mine, and I kiss his lips softly before pulling away slowly.

"No tongue?" He protests.

"Morning breath." I confess with a grimace.

"Next time I'll make you brush your teeth," he growls.

"Deal."

He descends the stairs while carrying me effortlessly, as if I weigh nothing to him. I want to tell him he doesn't have to carry me everywhere, but I don't think he would listen and it's pretty sexy. I could probably live with being carried by him for the rest of my life. When we reach the bottom, he sets me down, steadying me and reaching for my hand.

There is Christmas covering every square inch of this place. A giant tree greets me at the bottom of the stairs, decked out in glass ornaments. Its lights glow softly in the dim morning light. Another snowy day on the mountain and I already know I'm perfectly content to stay right where I am, except I wonder about the clause in the will that said I have to stay for a week. I could always extend my stay. I brought my work computer with me in case I got stuck up here. It wouldn't be unheard of, and my boss would never know. He has no reason to check on me so long as I get my work done. An extended vacation sounds nice.

Kane is tugging me past the tree and deeper into the house. There are nutcrackers, more garland, fresh wreaths, a Christmas village, and the entire house smells like the holidays. It's spicy, with the scent of the forest mixed in. Everything is perfect. In the kitchen, he seats me at a cozy little table and brings me over a muffin.

"Milk or cocoa, darling?" He asks, placing it in front of me.

"Cocoa," I grin.

"Good, me too." He kisses my hand, then leaves me to make hot cocoa. I continue to look around in awe at all the decorations. It's beautiful.

Kane slides in next to me a few minutes later, placing a cup of cocoa on the table in front of me. It's topped with whipped cream, dusted in cinnamon, and has what looks like crushed up gingerbread cookies on top.

"Wow, what is this? Are you some kind of famous chef or something?" I blurt out after I've swallowed my first bite of muffin.

"Or something," he teases. "Baking is just a hobby I picked up from my mom. She was a single mother and it was something we did together."

I reach out and squeeze his hand, popping another bite of muffin into my mouth. I didn't realize how hungry I was until I started eating. It feels like I haven't eaten in days. My mind drifts off with every bite I take. I'm starting to feel so much more awake. My body feels like it's buzzing to life after having been starved for sustenance. I try to remember last night and everything that happened, but all I can remember is the pictures and then my weird dream about having sex with Santa.

"What are you thinking about?" Kane asks, pulling me out of my head.

I bite my lip. I don't want him to know how weird I am, but I decide to tell him about my dream anyway. "If I'm being honest, I was thinking about a really weird dream I had last night where I was sleeping with Santa."

Kane grins. "Sounds sexy. If that's something you want to do, I have something we could both wear. I ordered a variety of sizes and choices because I was hoping you would turn out to be perfect. And now that I'm confessing this out loud, it sounds a little crazy."

"It doesn't sound crazy to me," I whisper. "I would love to play dress up with you, Santa." I wink.

Hazel

Chapter 22

We pull up in front of my uncle's place. I'm a bundle of nerves as I prepare to face Tyler. He really has some nerve coming up here and causing all this destruction to my property. I'm lucky Kane talked me into wearing our matching outfits and not to worry about what he thinks, because it doesn't matter.

Kane and I had some gingerbread cookies as a snack before we came down here and I brought a few with me for Tyler because he hasn't eaten since Kane tied him up and left him here. I take a deep breath as Kane rounds the truck to open the door for me and I slide out into his arms.

"You can do this," he says, encouraging me.

I offer him a smile. *How did I get so lucky?* I think, looking him up and down.

He's wearing nothing but a pair of red plaid boxers and a Santa jacket with a hat. The elastic on his waistband says naughty, which makes me blush. I'm wearing a sexy red dress with soft white fur lining that's entirely too short. My boobs spill out of the halter top, but I don't think Kane minds. He picks me up and carries me through the snow to the front door. There are only a few inches covering the cement. It's obvious he's been keeping up on the maintenance.

He sets me down on the step and I use Kane's property key to unlock the front door. He holds my hand as we walk deeper into the house to where Tyler sits tied up in the middle of the room in one of the kitchen chairs. Kane has covered him in rope, duct tape, and Christmas lights.

"Oh my god, Kane, are those Christmas lights?" I gasp.

He laughs. I thought you might get a kick out of that. "Is it too much?"

"No, it's perfect."

Tyler's head snaps up when he hears us talking. "You," he snarls at Kane.

"Get away from him, Hazel. He's a monster." Tyler warns.

"I think you're the monster, Tyler. You destroyed my uncle's house and murdered an innocent animal. And for what? To win me back? I'm not coming back. I'm never coming back. I am going to stay here for a while and live out my holiday romance happily ever after with Kane. Fuck off!"

His jaw drops in confusion and Kane runs his fingers up my arms in reassurance. I lean into his touch, loving the way it feels, like electricity crackling over my skin.

"You don't understand, Hazel. Let me tell you the truth." Tyler pleas.

"The truth, Tyler? Let's hear it. Entertain me." I bite.

"This guy, he paid me. He made me do it all. He made me cheat on you. He made me leave you to go to Florida, and he forced me to break your heart. I was going to propose to you, Hazel." He begs

I roll my eyes at him. What a sorry sack of shit he is. It took meeting a real man like Kane to realize what an actual piece of shit Tyler is. "I told you, Tyler, I will never forgive you for what you've done to me. So trying to blame Kane for your fuck-up is a low blow, even for you."

"It's true. You've got to believe me, Hazel. He threatened to kill me. He's a fucking psychopath. He drugged me, tied me up, and brought me here to kill me," Tyler shouts.

"You know what, Tyler. I've heard enough of your lies," I say, grabbing one of the gingerbread men I brought for him and shoving it in his mouth. "I think you're just jealous of what I found in Kane. Are you fucking jealous, Tyler?"

He can't answer and has no choice but to chew. I shove the second cookie in his mouth and place the empty plate on the coffee table. Then wrap my arms around Kane, kissing him hard and deep. I part my lips, allowing him to slip his tongue inside, and he doesn't hold back. He kisses me sensually until my body is bending to him and my brain is consumed with thoughts of fucking him right here in front of Tyler, just to prove my point. Kane's hand gives my ass an aggressive squeeze and I moan into his mouth.

"Let's make him jealous," Kane's voice is husky and low as his hot breath caresses the shell of my ear, his lips barely brushing against me, and sending tingles through my body.

"Kane," I whisper.

"Yes, darling."

I pull away, suddenly full of need as I stare up at him and into his Christmas tree eyes, through my thick heavy lashes purring, "I want you to fuck me in front of him. Make him understand I'm not his. I belong to you now, Santa."

"Fuck, Hazel." His words roll out of his mouth low and strung out. "I'll do whatever you ask me to. Is that really what you want?"

"Yes, Santa," I wink, feeling adventurous.

"Anything for you." He says, cupping my breasts as he kisses my neck while using his thumb to tease my nipples.

"What the fuck, Hazel?" Tyler shouts.

I ignore him.

"Tell him to shut up, darling, and to watch as I give you everything you could ever want." Kane says.

I spin around and Kane pulls my ass against him so I can feel his hard cock pressing into me, demanding my attention.

"Tyler, try to win me back then. This is your last chance." I purr.

Behind me, Kane stiffens, but I'm not worried. It will only make Tyler think he actually stands a chance.

Tyler tries, he clears his throat and begs. "Please, baby. Come to your senses. I don't know what he's said to you, but I swear to you, he did this. He threatened to kill me,

Hazel. It was the only way out he didn't leave me any options. I came back for you," he sobs.

I squeeze Kane's fingers and walk over to Tyler, bending over to give Kane a good view while Tyler gets a look at the girls hanging in his face. I reach a finger out, dragging it beneath his chin so he's looking into my eyes. Then widen my stance as if I am about to lower myself onto Tyler's lap. He looks at me wide-eyed and surprised. Then I drop to my knees in front of him and I'm sure he thinks I'm about to suck him off. I glance over my shoulder at Kane. He doesn't look happy. It gives me a rush of adrenaline. I turn my attention back to Tyler, and drag my hands across his thighs and sit back on my shins so I'm practically kneeling. He's looking at the ceiling, waiting for me to take him into my mouth, but that's not what is about to happen.

Chapter 23

Internally, I'm seething with rage as Hazel kneels before Tyler. I stare at her in disbelief at the turn in events. Externally, I do my best to maintain my composure, but given the smug look on Tyler's face, I must be doing a shit job of it. My fists clench and I clamp my jaw shut while fighting the urge to slice Tyler's neck myself, but I need

Hazel to do it. I have to know she's severed all ties and is committed to loving me.

She turns to look at me, and it's agonizing when she looks away. I take a long, deep inhale and try not to think about smashing his skull in. My jaw ticks. I'm ridiculously close to losing control. My vision is beginning to narrow as I glare at Tyler, sitting there thinking he's won.

Hazel looks back at me again, this time her eyes linger on me, sparkling with mischief. She's so fucking high, she's not going to remember anything but what I tell her when she wakes up. I just need her to figure out that I'm the serial killer because I really don't want to have to do the whole 'I need to confess something to you' thing this early in our relationship. I would really like to save that for later use.

She licks her lips as I search her eyes I can see how close she is to coming undone. She winks at me, then curls one finger at me.

"Come here and fuck me, Santa Daddy."

Oh hell yes! She's my fucking perfect little goddess, naughty in all the right ways. This girl is trouble, but I'm here for it. I'll do anything to keep her.

"For you, darling, anything." I growl. "But first I want you to crawl over here and suck Santa's big cock. Show him what a real man's dick looks like because, darling, that tight little pussy of yours needs to be stretched out from his tiny little dick."

"I want Tyler to watch me take a real man's cock," she groans impatiently.

"You will. But first I need you to get me hard."

Tyler scoffs, and I wink at him. I'm already hard, but it's not going to stop me from sweet-talking her into what I want.

"Don't do this, Hazel. Please untie me. I'll take us home. We can go back home together. Fuck this guy. Come on, baby." Tyler begs desperately.

"Tell him to shut up and watch, Hazel," I demand.

"Shut up and watch," she says, spinning in a half circle to wait for me as I walk to where she is. When I appear in front of her, I'm torn between watching Tyler's reaction, and the view of my girl sucking my cock. Tyler's reaction is a one-time opportunity. I'll never get to see it again, so I turn my head to glare at him smugly as Hazel's fingers work my waistband, freeing my dick. Hazel clasps it firmly and I hiss, pumping into her touch as Tyler's face drops. She licks me from base to tip, then circles her tongue over my head. She's going to have me coming if she keeps this up. The look on Tyler's face is priceless as she sucks me off. It feels great, the way her tongue drags across the throbbing veins of my straining cock. The pressure building in my balls tells me I'm going to release some pre-cum. As I feel it building, I time my thrust perfectly, holding onto her hair as I slam deep into her throat as my cock throbs, threatening to burst. She swallows saliva, and the sensation sends me over the edge as I'm thrusting into her throat. Hazel gags, but swallows my load down like the dirty girl she is.

I pull my cock from her mouth with a pop as her lips release it, then wipe the cum from her lips.

"You fucking win, Hazel. We're even. Now get up off the ground and untie me. You've proven your point." Tyler yells.

I grip him by the throat and squeeze as he gasps for air.

"No, stop." She says, her tone even and calm.

"I want you to fill me, Santa." She licks her lips. "I want you to show him how a real man satisfies a woman."

Yes. Anything for you. I think enthralled by her debauchery.

"Wait here," I growl, forcing myself to walk to the kitchen and retrieve some impromptu supplies.

I return carrying more Christmas lights and two packages of candy canes. "Let's show Tyler how much I've stretched that tight pussy out since I took over." Hazel giggles and gets on all fours. "Show him, Santa. Show him how many candy canes I can take."

"I'll show him how many candy canes it takes in place of my dick, and then I'll fuck you with them, so when I slip inside of that wet pussy, it tingles while I fuck you."

Tyler interrupts me. "You guys are fucking sick."

"Shut up, Tyler." Hazel snaps, standing up and walking to the kitchen to grab a knife.

Jesus fucking Christ, that escalated quickly. I really wanted to be buried inside of her when she murders him, but beggars can't be choosers, and I'll take what I can get so long as she's the one to end him.

She walks over to him, pressing the tip into his cheek until she draws blood. "I said shut up and watch, Tyler. Not another word from you."

"Hazel, please—"

"Not another word," she screeches.

He says nothing, hanging his head in defeat when she lowers the blade and places it on the ground next to where she gets back into position for me. "I'm ready for you, Santa."

That's my cue. I drop to my knees, watching Tyler as she lines herself up and sinks her hot, wet pussy right onto my head. I groan as her tightness surrounds me. She works me into her, sliding off and on my cock until finally her ass cheeks land against me and she's stuffed herself full. I thrust up into her, nice and deep until she's moaning for me. Tyler closes his eyes.

"Tell him to watch you come, darling," I growl, as her walls squeeze against me. "I want you to come for me while he's watching, Hazel. Be a good girl for Santa."

"Look at us," she demands, and when he doesn't, she lunges for the blade.

I move with her, not wanting to leave the warmth of her core. She stabs him in the foot and he screams, opening his eyes and watching as she comes around me.

"Such a good girl," I groan, thrusting into her and then pulling out.

I unwrap the candy canes and Hazel helps while Tyler whimpers in pain. Once all twenty-four are free from their wrappers, she gets back on all fours and waits. Tyler watches, obviously too afraid to look away as I lick each one, then slide it into her wet pussy. "How does that feel, darling?" I ask after sliding five in.

"I feel empty," she sulks.

"Do you need more to replace my cock?" I ask in a throaty voice.

"Yes," she pants.

I lick five more and insert them. "How's that?"

"Still empty, Santa. Give me more,"

Fuck, my girl is a filthy little tease. I'm never going to forget this. It's the best sex I've ever had. If this is what I get to spend the rest of my life doing with Hazel, I'll give it all up for this. I'll do anything she asks me. The voice in my head makes a whipping sound and I grin. I'll be as whipped as she wants for this pussy.

"Did you hear that, Tyler?" I taunt, mocking him. "She feels empty. She needs more. That's ten candy canes."

I lick five more and slide them in effortlessly, then reach around to rub over her clit with my sticky fingers. She grinds into them, panting.

"It feels so good the way it tingles," she gasps.

"Fifteen, darling. Do you need more?"

"Yes,"

I lick five more and slide them in. Her pussy accommodates them and she throws her head back in delight. "Don't stop. More."

"Shall I stuff you full of all twenty-four, since tomorrow's Christmas Eve and you've been such a naughty girl?"

"Yes, Santa."

I groan, licking them one by one and counting them out. "Twenty-one." Lick. "Twenty-two." Lick. "Twenty-three." Lick "Twenty-four."

I slap her ass. "How does it feel now, darling?"

"It feels just like when you're inside me." She moans.

"Did you hear that, Tyler? I've stretched her out enough to take twenty-four candy canes."

He huffs.

"Do you want me to fuck you with my candy canes like a good girl, Hazel?"

She nods her head.

"Use your words," I say, slapping her ass as punishment.

She yelps. "Please fuck me with your candy canes."

I want to piss off Tyler, so I coax her. "That's it. You like the way those candy canes feel just like me because you needed a big cock to fill you up and make you feel good. You needed a man who would put you on a throne and give you everything you could ever desire."

I reach around to rub her clit and she sinks deeper onto the candy canes.

"You fucking whore," Tyler shouts. He's had enough and I'm ready.

"Don't let him talk to you that way. Let's show him how you come on my dick."

I pull the candy canes out, and Hazel stands, surprising me.

"Can I have one of these?" She asks, pointing to the candy canes soaked in her cum.

I hand her one and she takes it to Tyler, stuffing it in his mouth and holding it there for a minute. Then she reaches for the knife on the ground.

It's really fucking happening. I shove a candy cane in my mouth, jealous she didn't give me one. I enjoy sucking her cum from it.

"Mmmm," I moan. "Delicious."

She smiles at me, then turns back to Tyler. She leans into his face. "Fuck off, Tyler. How dare you call me a whore. You're the only one here who has ever fucked a filthy little whore, and then you ran off with her and obviously have regrets. But it's too late for you, Tyler. You lost me for good."

She slams the knife into his thigh. Blood pours out. She severed his femoral artery. I grab Hazel, pressing her to the ground.

"Fuck me, darling. Show him what belongs to me now."

I wink at Tyler. He only has a few minutes before he bleeds out. Hazel spreads her legs, and I slam inside of her as he gurgles. I pump quickly, all the while staring at Tyler slowly fading away. I'm close and so is he.

"Roll those hips into me, Hazel. Make me come," I command, sliding my fingers through her wetness and around her clit to bring her over the edge with me.

It only takes a few more thrusts, and she's coming un-done around me. Tyler takes his last breath right as we come and it's a high I never once thought I would expe-rience. The adrenaline soars through my body, taking me deeper and deeper into my orgasm as I come harder than I've ever come in my life.

Tyler's fucking dead, and Hazel's all mine at last.

I'll take Hazel back to my place, clean her up, and put her to bed so she can spend Christmas Eve in my arms all over again. I want to fuck her sober so she can remember it this time.

Hazel

Chapter 24

Kane wakes me gently. His soft kisses cover my shoulders as his fingers trace up and down my spine. "It's time to wake up, my darling. You slept through breakfast and lunch. Wake up and join me for dinner." He kisses my neck and I moan.

I roll over to face him. "I'm so sorry."

"Don't be. You accidentally killed your ex-boyfriend Hazel. It's understandable you needed to sleep it off."

"I what?" she asks in horror.

"It was an accident. You couldn't have known you would hit his artery." Kane offers, trying to soothe me.

I brush a tear away.

"Hey, it's okay. I'll take care of everything. You just let me know what you want to do. We can talk about it at dinner. I ordered you a few dresses. I hope you don't mind, they're all green. It's my favorite Christmas color because it reminds me of the mountains," Kane confesses.

I smile, nodding my head. *I killed Tyler.* Right now, I want to throw up.

"Okay." I nod.

"Do you want me to help you dress, gorgeous?" He asks, as if he can sense my unease.

"Yes. That would be... nice. I'm not sure I want to be alone in my head. Will you talk to me while we dress? Distract me?"

"Go brush your teeth first and then I think I can handle that." Kane winks.

I stumble to the bathroom with Kane watching me. There are his and hers red and green towels. Candy cane print accent towels finish off the simple touch. The huge tub has garland dripping across the big window that tumbles down the sides. The twinkling lights give off a warm ambiance in the dusk-steeped lighting. Next to the tub, two embroidered towels hang engraved with the words Mrs. Claus and Mr. Claus. I cover my mouth. He's fucking perfect. *I just had to have a mental breakdown and murder my ex-boyfriend. What the fuck is wrong with me? How can he even still be interested in all this crazy?* I sigh, picking up a toothbrush from the crisp white marble countertops. A tube of toothpaste lay on the towel next to it and I pick it up next. As I brush my teeth, I turn around in the bathroom in awe. He must be a billionaire. Uncle Dexter's place is nice, but this house completely outdoes his.

"Hazel," he calls to me. "If you walk in the closet, you'll find the green dresses hanging up."

I spit and rinse, then take a deep breath before walking into the closet and screaming with excitement.

"I take it that means you like it?" He asks.

Not only has Kane retrieved all my clothes and put them away, he's filled the massive closet floor-to-ceiling with clothes in a variety of sizes for me. I wander to a shelf where green dresses hang and find one in my size almost immediately. He did a good job guessing. I'm betting he knew what I looked like from the funeral. *Oh god, did he plan all of this knowing exactly what I looked like? Could he have intended to try to convince me to fall for him? How fucking romantic.* I'm practically giddy, jumping up and down and silently screaming. I am the luckiest girl in the world. This man is my dream come true. *Could Uncle Dexter have known?* I feel tears threatening to spill out and blink them back. It doesn't matter, we found each other, and that's all I need.

I pick out two dresses and try them on, eventually settling on the second one. It matches the green bowtie he's wearing and the black velvet pencil skirt not only compliments his black suit, but is also short and sexy. Its hem falls perfectly, just low enough it covers the curves of my ass. The Christmas green corset top hugs my breasts with a sweetheart neckline that will surely drop him to his knees when he sees me. I walk out of the closet, giving him a spin.

"Will you lace me up, Mr. Claus?"

He laughs. "I know they are cheesy, but I didn't have a lot of options. When you accepted my invitation to stay up here for the week, I had to work quickly. I didn't know if you would want to transfer the ownership or just settle for the cash settlement."

"You're the lawyer, too?" I ask.

"Not a lawyer, estate manager." He corrects me. "Your uncle paid me handsomely to oversee the transfer of his estate to you."

My mouth gapes open. "Estate? I don't want to sound greedy, but do you mean I'm inheriting more than just his house?"

He pulls on the ribbon, gently lacing me into the corset, then tugs hard and ties it off at the bottom. His hands run over my shoulders and his lips move against my ear, whispering, "I'm going to be thinking about how goddamn sexy you look all night, Hazel."

I was wrong. It's me that's going to be melting to my knees. I could get used to his filthy mouth. I grab him by the chin, dipping his lips to meet mine. He's swallowing me in his embrace, his muscles melting me into him, as if we are meant to be one. Our bodies mold against one another and then his tongue is sliding against mine while his hands roam my body and I press my hand against the bulge in his pants. He strains into me, then pulls away, breathing heavily.

"Let's try to make it through dinner, darling, and then I'm going to rip that dress from your body and—"

I stop him. "No, please don't rip it. I love this dress. It's beautiful."

"I'll buy you a new one, darling." Kane brushes off my concern, like the money means nothing, and come on, it probably doesn't. I heard him. My uncle paid him a lot of money, and that's clearly not his only income stream.

"I don't want a new one. I want you to fuck me in this one, and then every time I wear it, you can remember tonight." I argue.

"Alright. Anything for you, dear." He bops me on the nose, then offers me his arm. "Shall we go have dinner?"

I loop my arm through his and allow him to lead me down the hall and back to the top of the stairs where he dips me. His kiss is just as deep as earlier. I can feel the tension burning between our bodies as they beg to be together. Kane's free hand runs up my thigh and pulls it closer to him, rotating my hip so I can feel his hard cock pressing against my pussy. I break our kiss first this time and whisper, "I'm not wearing any panties."

"Fuck, Hazel." He groans, drawing my name out the way he does that has my head swimming and my pussy aching for him. He slides his hand against my wet lips, dipping one in to stroke through my folds.

I moan. "You said we had to make it through dinner."

He releases me and leads me down the stairs. "That I did," He concedes, disappointment dripping from his words.

I smile, trying hard not to laugh at his sulking, but a soft chuckle escapes.

"What's so funny?"

"You're cute when you sulk," I tease him, running my fingers from the opposite hand over his arm that's hooked around mine.

He laughs. "Only because I think you mean it as a compliment will I allow this cuteness to go unpunished."

"Deal."

He leads me to the dining room where he helps me with my chair, then takes his place across from me. We do not sit at the head of the table, but rather across from one another. I'm guessing it's because he can't stop looking at me. In front of us are two plates covered by fancy silver lids to keep the food warm. He lifts the lid from my plate, and then his own.

"Beef Wellington. I hope you like it, darling."

I cut into the tender dish and it melts in my mouth. "This is amazing."

"I'm glad you like it. Merry Christmas Eve," Kane says, staring into my eyes.

"Merry Christmas Eve," I reply.

Over dinner, we discuss everything that happened yesterday. Kane offers to make it all disappear for me, as if it never happened, or to pay for a lawyer to represent me if I feel so burdened I want to turn myself in. All the while, he keeps repeating it was an accident, and that Tyler called me some horrible names. He tells me Tyler threatened to kill me just like the night when he showed up and chased me into the blizzard. He begs me to let him make it all disappear. I think he's right, though. No one needs to know, and it was an accident. There's no reason to put myself through that emotional trial when I will have to live with the guilt of what I did. It makes me feel so supported the way he's helping me through this.

When dinner is over, he leads me into the family room where he has a fire crackling and the tree lit up.

"Dance with me on Christmas Eve, darling. Make me a happy man." He pleads.

I can't say no. "Anything for you, right?"

He smiles, and I can tell it made his night. Hold on. Kane turns on Christmas on the TV with a Yule log burning as the background. Then places a pot over the fire to simmer. As it boils, the smell of Christmas fills the air, and the moment becomes absolutely magical as he wraps his arms around me, dancing to the music.

"You know, darling," he says casually. "If you'd like, I can arrange for Tyler to be taken care of and moved in with the others."

"With the others?" I repeat, confused. "Kane, you aren't making any sense."

He twirls me around then brings my fingers to his lips, kissing each one. "But darling, I'm making perfect sense."

He dips me and as my head falls back, my eyes land on a black ski mask, laying on the large leather sofa behind me.

When he pulls me back against him, he grips me tightly. "Yes, Hazel, there's something I need to tell you."

Kane

Chapter 25

"I'm a serial killer." I confess, placing my finger on her lips before she can say anything. "But Tyler lied to you. I don't want you to think any of that is true. It's been over a year since the last time I killed anyone, and I'm willing to give it all up to be with you. I've been giving it up, because I want to get better. I've done a lot of therapy, and I was going through some stuff after my mom died.

Anyway, your uncle, he was my person, my safe space, the one I called when I felt like I might relapse. Please. Hazel, tell me you still want to be with me."

"I still want to be with you. It's crazy, but I think we belong together." She cups my face. "I will let you take care of everything, but I do not want Tyler to become a part of your collection, and I would appreciate it if you could work on getting rid of the rest of them," she says using air quotes when she says the rest of them.

"I can do that for you, darling. It won't happen overnight, for obvious reasons. You know Christmas, and the fact that a bunch of perfectly preserved bodies can't just turn up without drawing a lot of attention."

"I understand." She lays her hand against my chest. "I think you should probably burn the bodies, and then we can both start over. It can be our little secret." She kisses my fingers, and it sends electricity pulsing through my body. I want her so badly in such a different way right now. I only want to worship her body, so she remembers every moment. It was important to me she accept me without the influence of drugs, and now that she has, I want everything to be perfect. I will love her for the rest of my life and I know I will never lay a single finger on her with the intent to harm her, because at our worst we were able to find love and recovery.

I mean, it's going to take some time to get rid of my collection, so a few more bodies anytime I get the itch shouldn't be a problem, and Hazel will never have to know. We can live happily ever after. Which reminds me.

"Hazel, darling," I say softly. "You've already made me a very happy man tonight, but well." I drop to one knee in front of the Christmas tree and present her with a black velvet box, pulled from between its branches. "I know it's soon and we've only known each other a few days, but in honor of holiday romances, would you do the honor of making our story perfect, and would you marry me? We can have as long of an engagement as you would like. I just can't stand the thought of you not having the respect of adorning my arm, without a big diamond ring on your finger to let all the other women know I'm your man, and I'm taken."

"Yes! Oh my god! Yes, Kane. How could I say anything but yes?" Her hand shakes as I slip the diamond ring onto her finger.

It's a perfect fit, just like I knew it would be when I looked up the size of the ring Tyler bought her. I scoop her into my arms, kissing her softly.

"Will you watch a movie with me, future Mrs. Claus?" I ask with a wink.

"Only if you promise to undress me first, because I was serious about the dress. I want to keep it to wear again."

"Darling, you can have anything you want. Money is no concern for either of us." He winks at me. "Heiress."

She grins and waits as I undress her first and then myself. Once I'm standing naked in front of her, we stand there examining each other until finally I tease her. "Do you see something you like?"

"I like everything I see," she purrs in response, dropping her gaze to my dick.

I can't wait to feel her nestled against me again. The way she melts in my arms feels like she was made for them. I sit down on the couch, patting to the spot next to me with one hand while the other grips my cock, stroking it. My sweet obsession is transfixed on me. She watches attentively as I glide my hand over my erection until a bead of cum drips out, running down my shaft.

"What are you doing?"

"Whatever you want me to be doing," I answer in a deep husky tone, reaching for the ski mask I intentionally left sitting out.

"So it was you that night?" Hazel asks, and I nod.

"I was hoping it was you." She blushes at her confession.

"Come sit on me," I demand, motioning with my finger.

To my surprise, she walks right over, straddling me, then slides her slick, hot pussy right onto my dick, impaling herself on my cock. This is exactly why my sweet candy cane was made for me and only me. Fuck you, Tyler. Finders keepers. I'm grinning and I know it's fucking sinister. Hazel takes it as encouragement, and I go right along with it.

My voice is soft, sultry even as I speak to her. "Well, look at that. You are a good girl."

"For you, Santa, always." She sinks herself until I'm filling her, then she rolls her hips rhythmically, slipping only the last few inches of my dick out of her, before slamming back down on my cock hard.

"If you keep that up," I moan into her mouth, "You're going to make me come."

"Good," she rasps, biting my bottom lip.

Bless her sexy ass, I've never wanted something as bad as I've wanted all of her right now, spent around me and orgasming, but I curse myself silently for my selfish desire to feel her just a little longer. "Just sit there. That's it. I want to make you cum one more time."

"Yes, make me come all over your big dick. You fill me up so good, Kane."

My name on her lips sends me over the edge. I'm just about to lose control, consumed by my desire. "Look at you," I rasp, sucking each one of her nipples into my mouth to tease.

When she can't stand the sensation, she pulls away, replacing her tits with her mouth. Her lips crash against mine like hungry waves, looking for a victim to devour, and it feels so good. My body buzzes full of adrenaline. She accepted me and we get to fuck like this for the rest of our lives. I've never felt more alive than I do right now.

Hazel's pussy squeezes around my cock. She's getting close again, and the way she's kissing me full of passion has my body screaming for me just to let go. My hands roam her body like a burning fire, then I bring one finger to stroke her swollen clit and use my other hand to guide her hip, setting the pace for her to ride me. Her tongue slips inside of my mouth as she swallows me in yet another kiss. Her pussy is wet and throbbing, soaking me in her cum.

My voice rumbles, "That's my good fucking girl. Come for me, don't stop."

She doesn't. She's soaking me and the couch. I'll buy a new one. I close my eyes and let her take me with her over the edge and into oblivion. As we cry out each other's names.

"Hazel."

"Kane."

"Hazel."

"Kane."

"Hazel. I fucking love you. You're perfect." I shoot my load deep inside her, filling her pussy.

"I love you too, Kane," she pants through her orgasm and then she's shaking in my arms and I hold her pressed against my chest as we both come down from the euphoria together. The grandfather clock strikes midnight, chiming.

"Merry Christmas, darling."

"Merry Christmas, my love." Hazel replies.

Acknowledgements

I have to thank my family for supporting me on this journey. Mr. Sweet puts up with a lot of research shenanigans from me and tolerates my anti-social writing sprints. My kids are always willing to distract me when I have a writing block, or help tape up boxes, and carry the mail.

A huge thanks to the entire team. Every single person involved with this process makes this possible. I am so grateful to have each of you on my team. There are so many readers who have helped me to grow my audience by sharing my work with friends. My ARC team as always you're amazing and I appreciate you so much for all the shares and shout outs.

I've also had the honor of working with several influencers for this release. I appreciate their willingness to collaborate in sharing about and promoting the release.

I should probably thank Joshua, for the photos and his willingness to jump on board with our team. He played hard to get for a very long time and it took a lot of convincing to get him to agree to them. His model cover is coming soon. We couldn't get the cover done on time but it will be available in the near future.

A special shout out to Kendra for earning the title of official vibe checker. We appreciate your developmental support and encouragement. A big thank you also to the entire vibe checker team. Thank you for reading early, and the crucial feedback you provided.

Finally to the A-Team. I can't do it without them. Jasmine and Megan thank you for all your help behind the scenes plotting feral and nefarious things. Megan requested a special recognition for her work on project: How Many Candy Canes. Thank you for sending pictures and videos to the group chat "Thumb to middle finger." as those measurements were imperative to the accuracy of the scene. Jasmine came to the rescue with a lesson on circumference and diameter, and together we can guarantee the candy cane math is solid.

As I am typing this we have officially surpassed 500 pre orders on this book and I am so incredibly humbled by every single one of you who ordered. This number means the absolute world to me. Thank you for helping me end 2025 with this insane accomplishment!

Mask Daddy Duet

You've just finished book 2 in the Mask Daddy Holiday Collection.
Have you read Underneath the Mask book 1 in the stand-alone series?

Coming Soon

Watch for Ringmaster March 2025 Pre Order Live Soon

More Holiday Books

Check out these additional holiday romances. Paws, Kisses, and Holiday Wishes Available for a limited time!

Baby It Snowed

Pawliday Love

About Des Sweet

Des writes deliciously dark romances in the contemporary and paranormal genres. Her books contain dark themes and characters in varying shades of morally gray. She's a sucker for the bad guy getting the girl. Demons, creatures, unalivers, stalkers, and mafia men frequent her pages. Her books might leave you with a new kink, or obsessing over a filthy mouthed book boyfriend. Popular tropes she enjoys writing include: enemies to lovers, forced proximity, and torture, in many different forms. Her name may sound sweet, but there's nothing sweet about the things she's writing, unless it's her morally gray contemporary romance line.

Looking for more content?

Join her reader group where you can find out how to order signed copies, chat about her books, meet other readers, and stay up to date on all the details for upcoming projects.

Des Sweet's Book Besties

Follow Des on REAM for FREE or become a member:

https://reamstories.com/dessweet

Interested in joining her Newsletter for first peeks, and exciting new releases or following her on social media? You can find everything you need in one convenient place:

https://linktr.ee/DesSweetWrites

Also By Des Sweet

Stolen Kisses

Ringmaster

Claiming Maeve

Gate 13